Skye Bird

and the

Eagle
Feather

by Mary Harelkin Bishop

Cataloguing in Publication data available
from Library and Archives Canada

ISBN 978-1-927570-39-5

Editing, book design and layout – Deana J. Driver
Cover and inside illustrations – Heaven Starr
Author photo – Mary-Jo Devine
Illustrator photo – courtesy of Heaven Starr

DriverWorks Ink gratefully acknowledges the support of Creative Saskatchewan's Creative Industries Production Grant program.

Printed on recycled paper. Printed and bound in Canada
by Houghton Boston Printers, Saskatoon, SK.

Published by
Emmbee Ink and **DriverWorks Ink**

Saskatchewan, Canada

DriverWorks Ink

110 McCarthy Blvd. N., Regina, Saskatchewan, Canada S4R 6A4

www.driverworks.ca   306-531-3171

Dedication

With much respect to Valerie Harper,
Saskatoon Tribal Council Director of Education.

You asked me to write a book like this years ago, Val,
but first I had and still have much learning to do
on my journey toward enlightenment and reconciliation.
With love to you and all of the First Nations children
growing up on Treaty Land.

- Mary Harelkin Bishop

Cree Dictionary

(All words from the Online Cree Dictionary)

Apisîs – little bit – Cheyenne's nickname
Awâsis – child
Kôkom – Grandma
Mósom – Grandpa
Okômâw – a great-grandmother
Wâpan – Dawn – Skye's mother's name
Witsana – relatives

Pronunciations

kôkom – ko-kum – grandma
mósom – mu-shum – grandpa

Chapter One

Skye Bird pressed her nose against the window as the school bus rumbled down the street and out of her neighbourhood. The kids, usually noisy and boisterous, sat quietly, some wondering, as Skye was, what would happen today. The decision to close their local school had been made in June and now it was September. School was starting again. Skye and the busload of students were heading to a big, shiny new school across town.

Skye's little sister, Cheyenne, impatiently pulled on Skye's shirt sleeve. "What?" Skye asked, turning to look down at her. Cheyenne was seven years old and going into Grade 2. Skye was in Grade 6 this year.

"What if I don't like my teacher?" Cheyenne asked for what seemed like the thousandth time.

"I'm sure she'll be nice," Skye answered, her voice and mind on autopilot.

"But she won't know me. She won't know what I'm good at."

"Well," Skye responded, parroting words she had heard her mother use over and over again during the summer, "you will just have to make sure to tell her all about yourself."

"Don't worry so much, Cheyenne," another voice said. Skye turned to smile gratefully at her best friend, Jamila, sitting in the seat behind. Jamila reached over the back of the seat and tugged playfully on Cheyenne's black braids hanging down her back. Jamila and Skye had been best friends since Grade 1, when Jamila's family had immigrated to Canada from Lebanon. At that time, Jamila didn't speak any English and Skye had taken Jamila under her wing, playing with her at recess and helping her learn to navigate the classroom and the school beyond. They had been inseparable right from the start and now Jamila and her parents were very good friends with Skye's family.

"But I liked our little school," Cheyenne persisted, her voice whiny. "Why did it have to close? There were lots of kids going there. I saw them every day," she reasoned, "so I know there were soooooo many." She stretched her arms wide, pinning Skye against the back of the seat.

Jamila and Skye both sighed. "Just not enough kids," Jamila answered as the school bus turned the corner and their new school came into view. It was so different from their old school. Even from the bus, Skye could see the two wings of the building leading out from the hub of the new school, where the front entrance and main office were located. She liked the look of her old school – a squat, two-storey little building with lots of windows and a fenced play area. The old school looked warm and inviting while this school looked huge and overwhelming.

The bus turned into the circular lane at the front of the school and stopped. "I hope you all have a wonderful day," the bus driver called as she pulled at the big lever and the door slid open.

No one on the bus moved. They stared out the small windows, watching as streams of kids and parents spilled up the wide walkway and rushed into the large school doors, loudly calling greetings to one another. It looked like sale day at the mall, Skye thought. She hated crowds. "Now that's a huge group of kids," she breathed quietly.

"Yeah," Cheyenne seconded, almost shrinking into the seat. "I've never seen so many people in my whole life."

"Stop being dramatic," Sage ordered, as he pushed down the aisle toward the front of the bus. "I don't know about you, but I'm going to really enjoy going to this new school! I can't wait to join the junior football team."

"Good for you, Sage," Skye said, feeling a pang of envy inside. Her brother, Sage, was already excited about this new school and was happy to be going to it. "Think of all the sports teams I can be on," he kept saying over the summer to anyone who would listen. Skye wished she could feel as eager as him.

Chris trailed along behind Sage, looking about as gloomy as Skye felt. He gave her a little smile of sympathy as he edged past her in the aisle and hurried after Sage. Chris was Sage's best friend and almost like a second big brother. He tried to like the things Sage liked, but Skye knew Chris wasn't excited at all to be going to this big new school.

"Let's go, kids," the bus driver called as Sage bounded down the steps and disappeared into the crowd. "You don't want to be late for the first day at your new school."

Gathering up her knapsack, Skye slipped the straps over one shoulder, then helped Cheyenne with hers. "Did Mom put my lunch in here?" Cheyenne asked, fiddling with the zipper.

"I'm sure she did," Skye answered. "Don't open it now, we have to go inside and find your classroom."

"Did she give me bannock? I asked her to." Cheyenne worried about everything these days.

"I'm sure she did," Jamila told her, taking Cheyenne's hand and helping her off the bus.

Together, the three girls made their way up the wide expanse of concrete sidewalk toward the front entrance of the school, trying not to be jostled by the other students. "Stay with me," Cheyenne begged, tears beginning to bulge in the corners of her eyes. Using both hands, she clung to Skye's waist. "I wish Mom or Dad could have come with me," she sighed. "Why didn't they?"

"You know why," Skye replied, tenderly patting her little sister's shoulder. "Mom couldn't get away from the Health Centre; everyone else is away at a convention or on holiday. You know she wanted to come with you; she felt really bad about it." Mom seemed stressed about work these days and that worried Skye. She worked on the reserve near the city. Dad worked at an alternative education centre for kids and adults.

"I know," Cheyenne sighed. "And Dad couldn't leave work either because he's giving the students a big, important exam to see if they can get their adult credit for high school."

"That's right," Skye agreed. Their father often had to administer tests for people. He also did a lot of teaching.

"Then you have to come with me," Cheyenne pleaded, digging her small heels into the sidewalk and pulling Skye to a halt, blocking the flow of human traffic into the building.

"I can't, Apisîs," Skye stooped down to hug her little sister, using Cheyenne's Cree name. It meant "little bit", and it suited Cheyenne perfectly; she was usually such a tiny, bright little thing.

"Walk me to my classroom, please," Cheyenne begged, clinging to Skye's hand as they pushed their way through the crowd of parents and kids and into the front doors.

"I will," Skye promised.

Even though they had been to this school twice

before, the front entrance still shocked Skye. It was massive and decorated to look more like a hotel than a school. The large foyer at the front of the school led to the big gym, library and main office, with the two long hallways branching off it as well. One wing housed the primary classes, where Cheyenne would be, and the other wing held the senior classes.

It felt a bit disjointed to Skye. She loved her old school, with its two floors of classrooms and several portables built on the end. It was old and worn, but it felt cozy and just right. Skye wondered if she would ever feel comfortable here. Pushing those thoughts away, she turned toward a large board which held the names of the new students. "Here's your name," Skye said, using her finger to trace an

invisible line across the page. "It says you are in room 10."

"What about us?" Jamila asked, scanning another board nearby for students in Grade 6. "Here I am," she said. Running her finger down the list, she frowned. "We're not together."

"What?" Skye asked, confused. "I thought we already knew we were in the same room. I thought they told us that we'd be together."

Jamila continued to search the list. "Nope," she said, her lips pursed together in frustration. "You're in room 23 and I'm in room 24. I'm really upset about this. I was counting on us being together."

"Me too," Skye sighed. "Maybe it's a mistake." She scanned the large expanse of the crowded lobby, looking for a teacher to talk to. "I'll see if I can find someone to ask."

The bell rang before Skye could move and the hall seemed to clear almost instantly. "I have to go!" Jamila called in panic. "I don't want to be late for my first day of classes!" Waving a hasty goodbye, she turned and hurried toward the wing where her classroom was, following large signs. "I hope you can figure this out, Skye," she called back over her shoulder. "I want to be in a class with you!"

Skye sighed. She didn't have time to be upset about herself and Jamila, she had to get Cheyenne to her new classroom. She had promised her mother she would look after Cheyenne today.

Half-dragging Cheyenne down the long hallway,

Skye easily found the room and pushed Cheyenne inside, but Cheyenne dug in her heels and leaned back against Skye's hands. "I can't go in there; I don't know anybody," she whispered.

"There must be one person from our school in your room," Skye responded, starting to get impatient. She had to get back to find someone who could figure out why she and Jamila weren't in the same room.

"I only see Charlie," Cheyenne stated. "He doesn't like me." As if to prove the point, Skye saw Charlie stick his tongue out at Cheyenne and roll his dark, shining and mischievous eyes in her direction.

"Well, at least he's in there with you," Skye sighed, ignoring Charlie's unfriendly behaviour. She hadn't realized how difficult it was going to be to get Cheyenne settled. It felt like it was taking ages and, in the meantime, the people in the hallway were quickly evaporating like dew in the hot morning sun. Soon, Skye felt sure, she would be the only student not in her classroom and that thought scared her.

"Cheyenne Bird?" a man's voice called from within the classroom.

When Cheyenne didn't answer, Skye said, "She's here," and firmly pushed Cheyenne into the room.

"Oh, good. My name is Mr. Patterson and I will be Cheyenne's teacher this year." He smiled and pointed to a desk. "You can sit there."

Looking like she was about to cry, Cheyenne slowly made her way across the room toward the last remaining desk. "You'll be okay, Apisîs," Skye called after her. "I'll see you after school."

"A-pee-what?!" a little, blond, curly haired boy called out in a rude voice. "Is that your name?" he demanded.

"Her name's Cheyenne," Skye retorted hotly, throwing a piercing gaze toward him. "And you'd better use it," she ordered. She kept her eyes on him until he bowed his head, staring at his desk.

Skye wondered when she had gotten into threatening little kids. But she didn't like the way he had tried to tease Cheyenne, and she had suddenly felt the need to make sure he knew Cheyenne had a protector. A protector? Skye shook her head. You really shouldn't need someone to protect you in Grade 2, should you? Didn't everyone just get along? Skye knew that Cheyenne had never had any trouble like this at their old school.

Feeling terrible about leaving Cheyenne on her own, Skye made her way quickly out of the room and back into the hallway. She had her own worries and getting herself to class soon was important. But first, she wanted to find out if there was some mistake about her and Jamila. Skye sprinted out of the long wing of primary classrooms and into the large, open, nearly deserted foyer. "Slow down, young lady," a firm voice called out. "It may have been okay to run through the halls at your other school, BUT it is not okay at this school. We expect respectful behaviour from all of our students."

"Sorry," Skye muttered as she screeched to a halt. "I don't want to be too late," she hastily explained to the woman who was standing with her hands on her hips. "And I also wanted to —"

"Then you should have gotten here sooner," the woman's voice coldly informed her. Skye looked into fierce blue eyes and gulped with fear. "I do not tolerate tardiness at my school. Now, which classroom are you looking for?"

"But—"Skye protested, wanting to explain how she had had to take her younger sister to school today.

"No 'buts' are allowed at this school," the woman stated flatly.

Sighing, Skye stepped in front of the tall, middle-aged woman with bleached blonde hair piled up on top of her head. She was wearing a name tag pinned on her left shoulder. It read 'Mrs. Miller' and Skye remembered that she was the principal. "I'm in room 23, Mrs. Miller," Skye practically whispered, her knees knocking together nervously.

"And what is your name?" Mrs. Miller asked, looking her up and down. Skye felt a disapproving gaze as the woman took in Skye's long, straight black hair, well-loved jeans and moccasined feet.

"I'm Sk-Skye Bird," she mumbled. "I was just—"

"Excuses are not tolerated nor are they expected." Mrs. Miller's terse response sent chills of anxiety coursing through Skye. "Do better next time. I will be watching you." Mrs. Miller emphasized the words so strongly that Skye was sure she would be under close inspection and it made her even more nervous. Abruptly ending the conversation, Mrs. Miller turned sharply on her heel, leaving Skye standing in the middle of the deserted foyer feeling about a centimetre tall, and she hadn't gotten the chance to ask about why she and Jamila weren't in the same classroom.

That woman's cold gaze was scary, Skye decided, and she hoped she wouldn't have to have any more to do with her. At her other school, the principal was warm and friendly. He was always in the hallways, greeting and teasing the students and asking if they'd had a good day. Skye didn't think for a minute that Mrs. Miller did that kind of thing and it made her feel sad. Would she ever grow to like this new school?

Chapter Two

Trying to collect her self-confidence, Skye took a huge breath and turned down the senior wing of the school, searching out her room number. Why wasn't she with Jamila, in the same room? Her old teacher had assured her that they would try to make sure everyone had a friend or two in the new classroom. She had even made them list the names of kids they would like to be with. Skye sure wished she was with Jamila. It would make this transition so much easier.

Room 23 loomed ahead and Skye stopped at the door, peering inside. She saw several kids from her old school and she was glad. There was Miranda Whitehead, Raven Poorman, Justin Greyeyes, and Tyrell LaVallee. They weren't best friends or anything, but they did like each other and hung out together sometimes. Skye must have made a faint noise; they all looked up, threw weak smiles her way and then went back to hunching up in their desks as if they were trying to be invisible. "Mrs. Bone" was written on the whiteboard and, judging by the tall, gangly, grey-haired woman standing at the front of the classroom, Skye decided it was a fitting name. "You must be Skye Bird," a voice interrupted Skye's thoughts.

"Y-yes," Skye stammered.

"Well, don't just stand there. Come in and take a seat."

Skye glanced around the room and saw one remaining desk open on the far side of the classroom. It was the first desk in the last row against the windows. At least she could look outside, Skye thought as she slowly made her way toward it. Her face grew hot as she felt everyone staring at her, except for the kids she knew. They weren't looking at her at all.

"I will continue with the rules of the classroom," Mrs. Bone stated. She stopped and stared pointedly at Tyrell. "Rule Number One – no baseball caps are to be worn in this classroom or anywhere in this school."

"Aww, man," Tyrell groaned, his fingers reaching to touch the green-and-white Riders cap that sat on his head. Reluctantly, he slid it off his head and into his desk.

"But we could wear them at our other school," Justin called, pulling the Oilers cap from his own head.

"Rule Number Two," Mrs. Bone continued as if neither boy had spoken. "No speaking out in class. You need to raise your hand."

Tyrell raised his hand, but Mrs. Bone ignored him. "Rule Number Three," she continued.

"Can we at least discuss it?" Tyrell complained loudly.

"You are interrupting, young man," Mrs. Bone said, pointedly. "You are being disrespectful." The class snickered around them.

"You say I can only speak if I raise my hand. I raise my hand, but you don't call on me; so now I'm speaking out. I think we should be allowed to wear our hats in school." Tyrell was being really brave and brazen, Skye thought. She silently applauded him.

"No hats," Mrs. Bone said firmly, "and if you speak out of turn again, I will send you to the principal's office."

"Ohhh," the other students in class chorused, "in trouble on the first day!"

Raven, sitting in the desk behind Tyrell, reached over to touch his arm and shush him. Skye could see Raven shaking her head at him and he quieted down as Mrs. Bone continued. "Rule Number Three, tardiness in the class will not be tolerated. Rule Number Four, keep your hands and feet in your own space at all times. Rule Number Five, you must ask for permission to leave the room, go to the washroom, or leave your desk. Are the rules clear?"

Most kids nodded in agreement. Skye sighed. This felt more like a prison than a school.

"Now," Mrs. Bone announced, folding her hands together. "In order to get to know one another, we are all going to all stand up, say our name – both first and last – and tell one thing we did this summer and one special thing about ourselves." Turning, she picked up a marker in her bony fingers and wrote the instructions on the board, as a reminder to the students. "And we will start here," she said, pointing right at Skye.

Skye felt her stomach lurch as her heart kicked up into triple time. She hated being first with anything and this was awful. What would she say? Slowly, she stumbled to her feet, her mind whirling. "Uhh ... my name is Skye Bird," she mumbled, staring at the desk in front of her.

"You must speak up," Mrs. Bone ordered. "Try again."

"My ... my name is—" Skye tried to speak more loudly, but her lips were glued together with terror and her tongue felt numb and useless.

"You must speak up," Mrs. Bone repeated once again. "Try again, and louder this time."

A few of the other students snickered and Skye flushed, feeling heat flood her cheeks. "My name is—"

"You must be louder," Mrs. Bone interrupted again. "How can you expect the other students to hear and get to know you? Try again and, rest assured, I will keep interrupting you until you get it right. It may seem mean to you now, but it's for your own good."

Skye could feel heat rise up to her hairline as tiny

beads of sweat popped out on her forehead and upper lip. She wished with all her heart that she could dive out the window and run away. Already, she hated this school and this teacher. Every eye in the classroom was on her and she felt caught in a snare like the ones her mósom used when he trapped small mammals in the winter. A few kids smirked and snickered at her. One boy even stuck his tongue out and crossed his eyes, pointing at her.

I can do this, Skye willed herself, closing her eyes and taking a shaky breath. I WILL do this because I don't want to have to start again! Gathering her strength, she started again, feeling like she was shouting. "My name is Skye Bird and I spent a lot of the summer at my grandparents' cabin at the lake. One special thing about me is that I dance tap, jazz, and powwow. We had a powwow dance group at our school, so I'm going to join the one at this school too." Relief made her limbs weak and she flopped into her seat like a wet noodle.

"Next," Mrs. Bone called.

Skye blanked everything out after that. She didn't catch one kid's name and she sure didn't learn anything about any of them. She just sat in a puddle of humiliation, wishing the floor would open up and swallow her. This was the worst day of her life.

The first part of the morning passed on turtles' legs, slow and endless. It seemed an eternity until the recess bell rang. Relieved, Skye slowly got to her feet, letting the other students leave the room before her. No one bothered to wait for her or smile in her direction. She was happy to look up and see Jamila's face peer into the empty classroom.

"There you are," Jamila said, coming in and taking Skye by the arm. "Let's go outside and see what's what." Happily, and feeling very relieved, Skye let Jamila lead her outside and into the warm, morning sun.

Even though it was September, the heat of the summer persisted and Skye wished they were back at the lake with her Mósom and Kôkom. She loved spending the summers at their cabin. They told stories about being young and Skye learned many words in Cree. The whole family went on berry-picking expeditions and Mósom took Skye and Sage fishing, where they each caught their first fish. She wondered what her grandparents were doing today. Did they miss having their grandkids around?

"How's your classroom?" Jamila asked.

Skye shrugged. "Okay, I guess," she said, choosing not to tell Jamila about her horrible experience. That would only make it more real and Skye didn't want to talk about it right now; it was too painful. "Nobody talks to me or even looks at me. It feels very weird here at this school. But I am in the same classroom as Tyrell, Miranda, Raven, and Justin. I'm just sorry you're not in there with us. I tried to ask the principal about the mix-up, but she kept interrupting me, so I never got the chance. It feels very weird here – sort of, I don't know, unfriendly, I guess."

"I know what you mean," Jamila replied. "They're telling us all these rules and they're acting like we were wild animals at our other school or something. They keep looking at us new kids like we have horns growing out of our heads."

Three girls from Skye's class sauntered by. One was Miranda and Skye turned to smile at her, but Miranda ignored her. "Isn't that the girl that said she dances powwow?" one of the girls laughed.

"Yeah," another replied. "Whoever heard of a powwow group at school? That'll never happen here!" They all burst out laughing, hooked arms and walked away.

"Yeah," Miranda agreed, loudly, tossing her head. "Who likes to dance powwow anyway?"

The girls laughed again, but Skye gasped. "Miranda loves to dance powwow," she burst out. "She's the best Ladies Traditional Dancer I know!"

Jamila shook her head. "I think she's just trying to fit in with those other girls and be their friend, though I don't know why. They were all so rude."

"Yeah, I noticed that too, and it's directed at me. They don't even know me, but they sure don't like me," Skye said sadly. "And the principal, Mrs. Miller – wow – stay away from her. She's scary." Skye searched the large playground area. It was on a big square, with mature spruce and elm trees bordering the edges. The trees provided shade on hot days and gave the students a place to play or talk quietly under the ample branches. "I should go see how

Cheyenne's doing," Skye said, searching the trees, sure she would find Cheyenne hiding under one of them.

"I see her," Jamila pointed next to the school's wall. She was playing with another small girl. They were tossing a ball back and forth between them. "At least she seems to be making friends."

"I think it's easier when you're younger," Skye replied. Cheyenne looked up to see Skye and Jamila. Dropping the ball like a hot potato, Cheyenne tore across the busy play area and flew at Skye, enveloping her in a bear hug. "Not so hard," Skye protested, prying Cheyenne's arms away. "You're hurting me."

"Sorry," Cheyenne said, releasing her hold and grabbing Jamila instead. "I'm just so glad to see you guys!"

"It looks like you've made a new friend," Jamila pointed out, laughing as she returned the hug.

"Yeah, she's okay. I like her. Her name is Brandi and she's new too. She woulda gone to our old school, 'cepting it's closed now."

Brandi stood against the school wall, looking lost and forlorn as she bounced the ball in front of her. "I think you'd better go back, Apiŝîs," Skye said. "It looks like your friend needs you."

"Okay," Cheyenne agreed. "See you later." And with one more hug each, she skipped back across the schoolyard to Brandi.

"Oh, if only life could be that easy," Skye sighed and Jamila laughed.

"It's not that bad," she said, smacking Skye on the arm. "I'm sure we'll get used to it," she said as the bell rang, beckoning the students back inside.

"I hope so," Skye said, and she and Jamila parted ways.

The rest of the day was full of learning new procedures and getting used to a new teacher's ways. Mrs. Bone seemed to repeat things many times, and the little bit of writing she asked them to do was nothing to Skye, who was used to writing stories and long research essays. Skye finished in a matter of minutes and spent the rest of the time doodling at her desk. She tried to stay invisible. That was the best way to be, she decided.

That evening, when Mom asked her how school went, Skye shrugged. "Okay," she lied. Mom had enough worries and Skye didn't want to add to them. Mom wasn't fooled though.

"Are you sure?" she asked. "I want you to be happy."

"I know," Skye said, hugging her mom. "I think it'll just take some time to adjust to things."

Mom nodded, "You're right."

"What about you, Apisîs?" Mom asked, pulling Cheyenne onto her lap and cuddling her. "Did you like school today?"

"I liked a lot of it. I made a new friend, Brandi. She

has a puppy and she says I can come over to see it sometime. And we painted pictures and we get to bring them home tomorrow when they're dry. I'm going to hang mine up in my bedroom. And we went to the library." Suddenly Cheyenne got quiet.

"And?" Mom prompted. "How was it?"

Cheyenne wrinkled her nose. "It was kinda good and kinda bad."

"Why was it bad?" Skye asked.

"Because I couldn't find my favourite book. I've been waiting all summer to read my favourite book again and they don't have it at the library. They don't have any of my favourite books at that library."

"You mean *Red Parka Mary*?" Skye asked. She knew Cheyenne's special book; she had read it to her and with her many times last year.

"Yeah," Cheyenne said. "I asked the librarian. And they don't have that book. Then I asked for my other favourite book, *When We Were Alone*, and they didn't have that book either.

"Maybe someone else had them signed out," Mom said.

Cheyenne shook her head firmly. "No; I asked. The librarian said those kinds of books make people sad and why did I want to read them. Then she gave me a different book to sign out." She shrugged her shoulders. "It's okay, but it's not my favourite."

"I'm sorry about that," Mom said, looking worried, but she was interrupted by Sage.

"School's going to be great!" Sage said, bounding into the living room and bumping down on the couch. They posted all of the clubs and sports teams and I've signed up for some, but I really want to play on the junior football team."

"You'll be great on the team, Sage," Dad said, sitting down beside him. "We'll make sure to come to all your games too." Dad ruffled Sage's hair.

"Did you join Culture Club?" Skye asked, "Or the Drumming Group?"

Sage frowned. "I didn't see those things on the list. It's just a lot of sports things like cross-country and volleyball, basketball, some kind of fitness club, music and art clubs. I guess they don't do Culture Club and Drumming at this new school."

"No?" Skye questioned in surprise. Culture Club was one of her favourite groups. It was a school-wide group at the old school, with kids from almost every grade level. The group planned and organized events to help everyone get to know everyone's culture. They had even started an event called "Friendship Night". It was an evening when parents came out and brought a potluck food item. Every-one was invited to share and mingle. Anyone, even parents, could perform a dance or sing a song. Some people made PowerPoints and talked about their culture or the country they had come from. Skye loved this because not only new Canadians came to the event, many First Nations families came too, as her family always did. They told stories or shared something special about their culture or something unique to their own reserve. And, of course, there was drumming and powwow dancing.

"What about powwow?" Skye asked, a sinking feeling in her stomach. "Did you notice a powwow group?"

Sage shook his head. "Nope. I didn't see that either." He shot a sympathetic look at his sister. "You'll just have to join different groups, I guess."

"But I loved dancing powwow and you loved learning to drum," Skye protested. The thing she loved most about it, besides learning all the dances and getting to wear beautiful regalia, was that anyone could join powwow, and many people did.

Jamila danced powwow and so did many of the other new Canadian kids. They loved it.

"What about the drumming group?" Skye added. At their old school, boys of all ages and nationalities joined the drumming group. Sometimes watching them drum felt like watching a United Nations festival; at least that's what Skye's dad always said, with a smile on his face.

"What are we going to do without those things? How will school ever be fun?" Skye sighed, a feeling of unhappiness dragging her sad heart into the pit of her stomach.

That night, Skye went to sleep worrying about school and worrying about Cheyenne not having her special books to read. In the night, she had a dream. An old woman came to her and said, "My name is Okômâw. I am a great-grandmother to you. I will teach you and help you. And remember, you must always be true to yourself."

The dream faded as the morning grew light. By the time Skye awoke, the dream had almost disappeared from her memory.

Chapter Three

Skye continued to struggle at school. Even though she tried, she was not happy. Mostly, she worried about Cheyenne. Her usually bubbly and happy little sister was becoming a shadow of herself. She did what she was told, brought home a library book every night and read it with Mom or Dad or Skye, but she didn't delight in the books as she had with her favourite stories.

When Skye's class went to the library, she purposely looked for the books that Cheyenne wanted, but they weren't listed in the online catalogue. Curious and puzzled, Skye searched the library shelves for book titles she knew, like *Walk Two Moons* by Sharon Creech and *Road Allowance Kitten* by Wilfred Burton. She couldn't find them.

"Can I help you find a book?" the librarian asked.

"I'm looking for books about Cree people, or the Métis. Where are they kept?" Skye asked, looking around. At her old school, the books were always on display and had their own large shelf in the library.

The librarian studied Skye's brown skin and black shiny eyes and hair, then looked away. "We really don't have much; just some older books with historical content that are used when classes research First Nations."

Skye flushed, annoyed. Her culture and history were important; she was a person! "I just wanted to read a book about my People's history – their REAL history!" she said.

"Sometimes those books are upsetting to readers, so we just don't keep them in this library," the librarian said stiffly. "We don't want to upset anyone."

"Well, it's upsetting me that I can't find any books about people like me in this library. Don't I count too?" Skye blurted out before she could help herself, her tone sounding disrespectful. "And what's wrong with reading books that might make you sad? They also make you learn something. And most of them are about the history of the People! My people!" By the time Skye finished speaking, her voice had risen several decibels and everyone in the library stopped in their tracks, staring at her.

The librarian huffed and pointed a long finger toward the door. "This is a quiet place for serious students with serious requests. Come back when you can be the kind of student we want to have here in this school."

Angrily, Skye stomped across the room and threw open the door, letting it bang against the wall behind her. Raven and Justin gave her a thumbs-up sign as she walked by them and she couldn't help but give them a triumphant smile, but she felt deflated inside. All she wanted was to read books about her history and her own people. So why did she feel like such a criminal?

Skye stood seething in the hallway, waiting for her class to finish getting their books. Sage appeared out of nowhere, surrounded by his new friends, heading out to the front of the school to play football. "What did you do now?" he hissed at Skye as he strode past.

Skye shrugged. "I just asked for books about us – about our kind of people – and they don't have any."

"Forget about those books," Sage warned her. "Just read something else, or don't read at all. You need to learn to fake it to fit in here, like me. You need to get along with everyone, Skye, or life will be hard for you." Sage turned and followed his friends outside to play ball.

Life is hard, Skye thought miserably. It didn't seem to matter what she did, life was difficult. She just didn't know how to fit in. She didn't know how to let things go, like Sage did. Maybe she should try harder to do things his way. It sure seemed to be working for him.

Although Skye tried to fit in, it just didn't feel right and her heart always felt heavy with sadness. Whenever she looked at Cheyenne, she saw that same feeling mirrored in her eyes. One night after reading together, Skye said, "Tomorrow after school, why don't you and I walk down to the public library and get the books you want to read?"

Instantly, Cheyenne's eyes lit up. "Oh, can we?" she cried, jumping up and clapping her hands. "I would love that. I miss my stories sooooo much." She opened her arms wide and fell back against the sofa.

"I know you do," Skye said. "I'll ask Mom if we can walk from school instead of taking the bus home. Maybe she or Dad can pick us up afterward. Maybe Jamila can come along with us."

"Yes, that would be wonderful!" Cheyenne clapped her hands and whirled around.

"You're a drama queen," Skye laughed.

"So what? I'm happy," Cheyenne said simply, and Skye couldn't argue with that.

Mom agreed, and Skye texted Jamila to invite her to go to the library with them.

Skye: What's up?

Jamila: Not much. Just doing homework.

Skye: You get homework?! I don't. It's weird.

Jamila: That is weird. My teacher keeps telling us we need to work hard to be successful in grade 7-8-9.

Skye: Weird. Do you want to come to the public library with Chey and me after school tomorrow?

Jamila: Wait, I'll ask.....Yes!! Yay!

Skye: Great! I'm glad! C u soon!

Jamila: Yep! Xoxo :)

Skye frowned as she put her phone down. School had been going on for several days now and she hadn't gotten any homework yet. Not that she wanted it, of course! It's just that, it never felt like she was learning anything new in her classroom either. Mrs. Bone didn't seem too interested in teaching them much. It was mostly short assignments or a few questions out of the Math textbook. Just to keep busy, Skye often did more questions than were assigned. This didn't seem to bother the other kids, but it did bother her.

And reading – Skye loved to read! It was one of her favourite things to do, but this teacher insisted that she read these little short stories on computer and answer five or six really boring questions. Sometimes she cheated and answered the questions before she read the story! She was smart enough to figure out the answers and always moved up to the next level. Last year, at her old school, the students had gotten to choose the novels they wanted to read, and they discussed things like common themes running through the books, or how the characters changed from the beginning of the story to the end. Skye missed that.

She missed the inquiry projects they did last year too. She loved it when her brain felt busy and full of new knowledge just bursting to be shared with everyone. That's what inquiry learning did for her. That was when she felt like she was learning the most, and that was when school was really fun. At this new school, what Skye felt most was bored. She sighed. She really, really missed her old school and teachers. She missed learning.

After school the next day, the girls met outside the front entrance. Skye got there first and found Chris leaning against the building. "Hey, Chris."

"Hey," Chris replied, not looking happy.

"What's wrong?" Skye asked.

Chris shrugged his shoulders, then pointed to the boys playing touch football on the front lawn. Sage was right in the middle of the pack, enjoying every second of it. "Not much. I just don't like it here and I'm not into football, like Sage. It's not the same here, you know. And Sage is already on so many sports teams. I'm missing our old school, our groups, our laughs."

"I know," Skye said. "I haven't signed up for any groups here yet either, even though the teacher keeps asking me to. I told Mrs. Bone that I wanted to join something like our old clubs – you know, the Culture Club and our Powwow Group."

"And what did she say?" Chris asked.

Skye shrugged her shoulders. "She told me to take another look at the list and join something they were already offering here. She said I was being difficult and I should try harder to fit in."

"And?" Chris prompted her to continue.

Shrugging her shoulders, Skye leaned against the warm brick of the school building. "There's not much I want to join here. I'm not really into sports, you know, but I feel pressured to join something."

"Me too," Chris said, bumping the toe of his running shoe against the school wall. "I just want there to be a Culture Club and Powwow, you know? We had so much fun with those clubs last year."

"I know," Skye said. She, Chris, and Jamila had been in the Powwow Group together. Skye was a jingle dancer, Jamila was a fancy dancer, and Chris was a grass dancer. Sage used to dance, but now he drummed. "I wonder what happened to all of our regalia. Do you think it's still at the old school? I wonder who I could ask."

Chris shrugged. "I don't know. Nobody here seems to even care about what we did at our old school. They just want us to fit into this school."

"Yeah," Skye agreed, "and do what they say, and act like them. It makes me feel weird."

"Yeah, I don't know how Sage does it, but he does.

He just pretends to be somebody else. Sometimes I don't recognize him, you know. But everyone here seems to like him," Chris said, watching as some of the boys clapped Sage on the shoulder.

"I wish people liked me more," Skye muttered. "Miranda seems to be able to do what Sage does too. She's made some friends in our classroom. I wish I could figure out how."

Chris scoffed. "I've seen Miranda around here trailing after those girls. I don't think they're really her friends. She's not acting like herself, either. Don't change to suit them, Skye. Just be yourself."

Startled, Skye looked up into Chris' eyes as her dream flooded back into her brain. Hadn't the old kôkom in the dream said those very words? What was her name? Skye tried hard to remember – oh yes, the old woman had said, "My name is Okômâw." And now Chris was telling her the exact same thing. It was freaking her out!

Jamila and Cheyenne came bustling out of the school doors together and the dream disappeared. Chris walked with them partway to the library, then turned down a street to walk home. "Remember what I said, Skye," Chris repeated as he walked away. "Be true to yourself."

Skye thought about Chris's words as she got into bed that night, then she remembered the dream again. She knew visions were important in her culture – they were a way to help a person learn something, and Skye knew she needed all the help she could get. Should she listen to Sage? she wondered, as she snuggled down under her cozy blanket. He seemed to have it all figured out and it sure was working for him. He was very popular at school. Everyone loved to have him on their team and he was always at the centre of everything. Or should she listen to Chris, who told her not to change just so people would like her? Had Sage changed? In a way, he had, she thought. He was giving up things he loved to do, like drumming and playing at powwows. Did he even mention these things to his new friends?

Tossing and turning, Skye tried to get comfortable; she tried to turn off her brain, but thoughts and words kept spinning around in her mind like irritating mosquitoes bombarding her head. She punched her pillow a time or two and turned it over. Her hand brushed something hard beneath and she searched to find one of Cheyenne's library books they had borrowed from the public library. It was one of the stories about residential schools. Placing the book on her night table, Skye put her head back down on her pillow, thinking about the story. The children weren't allowed to have their own culture. They weren't allowed to be themselves. They were forced to be like everyone else.

Was that what this school was trying to do? Skye wondered as she drifted off to sleep. Not in a bad way, really, but in some ways, it seemed like it. By not having the kinds of books Cheyenne wanted and needed to read, that was a way of forcing everyone to be the same. And by not having Culture Club and Powwow Group, wasn't that another way of making sure everyone did the same things? But maybe it wasn't so bad. After all, they could easily get those books from the public library. And as for the other things, well, Skye just didn't want to cause trouble. And anyway, she was already seen as a bother. She just wanted to fit in and be like Sage. That seemed the best way to be and Skye decided that was what she would do.

Okômâw came to Skye in another dream. She smiled at her and brushed her hand against Skye's cheek. "Awâsis ... My Child... you have a lot of worries. You must be strong," she murmured. "You see what is happening and you know what is right. I will be there to help you. Watch for me." Her voice faded away and, in the dream, Skye watched as Okômâw drifted off into the darkness, clutching an eagle feather in her hand.

When Skye woke in the morning, the dream lay heavy on her mind. She could see Okômâw clearly, the eagle feather still clasped in her hand. It was a large and beautiful feather. With a long, graceful, slight curve, it was pure white for about two-thirds of the length of it, but the top third was dark black, and it looked soft to touch. Most of all, Skye could hear Okômâw's voice telling her she must be strong.

Skye didn't want to be strong; she just wanted to fit in. She decided to ignore Okômâw and the dream; she climbed grumpily out of bed as Mom called her from the kitchen.

"Are you up yet, Skye?' Mom yelled. "You're going to be late for the school bus!"

"Coming!" Skye yelled back. She hurriedly tossed the covers onto her bed and jumped into some clothes. "I'll be down in a minute!"

"I'm having cereal for breakfast," Cheyenne reported as Skye burst into the kitchen.

"So is Skye," Mom decided, plunking a bowl of Corn Flakes down in front of her and splashing on some milk.

"Thanks, Mom." Skye decided not to argue.

"Mom, what does 'Okômâw' mean? I think it's a Cree word."

As Mom thought for a moment, Dad came into the room. "It is a Cree word," he acknowledged. "It means great-grandmother."

Skye nodded, thinking of Okômâw's image from her dreams. "So, like, someone who's really, really old?"

"Yes, I suppose so," Dad answered, pouring himself a cup of coffee. "Why are you asking?"

Skye studied her father as he stirred sugar into his coffee and popped bread into the toaster. He was a handsome man with a long, neat braid hanging down his back. He always wore a crisp dress shirt and dress pants, and a necklace or medallion suspended from his neck. Today, he wore a stone arrowhead he had found in a field on the reserve and had made into a necklace.

"I've been having dreams ... visions, I guess," Skye answered, slurping up her cereal.

"Really?" Both parents looked expectantly at her, waiting for her to continue. Neither was surprised, since visions with messages happened a lot in their family. "Are you worried about something?" Mom asked, placing her hand on Skye's shoulder.

Skye shrugged just as a horn sounded from outside. "Oh, the school bus!" Cheyenne interrupted, dashing from the table. "Come on! We're going to be late!"

There was a mad scurry of confusion as the kids grabbed their lunches and backpacks and swept out the front door. Skye gratefully left Mom's question unanswered. It wasn't that she was worried about just one thing. She was worried about everything!

Chapter Four

Sage was already on the bus as Cheyenne and Skye raced down the front steps toward the street. The bus door was wide open, beckoning the kids aboard. Skye watched as Cheyenne mounted the steps and waved happily at someone. Skye was sure it was Brandi. Slowing her steps, she ground to a halt, her stomach turning somersaults faster than a gymnast. "I ... uhh ... I forgot something," she lied, backing away from the bus. "It's important and I have to go get it."

"I can't wait for you," the bus driver commented, looking pointedly at her watch. "I have others to pick up."

"That's okay," Skye said. "My ... uhh ... my parents will drive me." As if to prove her point, her mother stepped out onto the front step and closed the door behind her.

"All right," the bus driver said, glancing toward the house. She snapped the door closed and the bus rumbled away with Skye rooted to the sidewalk.

Skye spied Jamila's wide-eyed look of horror as the bus turned the corner and disappeared.

Without thinking, Skye dove down behind the fence, crouching behind a small lilac bush growing near the sidewalk. Mom, always in a hurry, didn't even glance her way as she backed the car out of the driveway and headed for work. Skye knew Dad would be coming soon so, not wanting to be discovered, she bent over at the waist and ran to the end of the block, where a copse of trees in a little wooded park invited her in.

What have I done? Skye wondered in fright, her heart still thudding loudly against her chest. She hadn't meant to skip school; it just happened. But she felt relieved. She couldn't stand school right now. She missed everything about her old school. She knew she'd be in trouble but, at the moment, all she felt was a pure sense of blessed relief.

Walking along the paths of the little wooded area her family optimistically called The Forest, Skye felt happy. The trees stood tall, their leaves and branches hiding her from view. On the far side of The Forest was a small boulder standing about a metre tall. A plaque at its base described it as a buffalo rubbing stone. Trees had grown up around it over the years and it blocked her view of a gently sloping coulee leading down to the river which flowed nearby. In her imagination, Skye could see the millions of bison grazing on the prairie grass. She also knew that across the wide river, on the high cliffs, were bison jumps where her people had stampeded bison. Her phone pinged suddenly, bringing her abruptly back to reality. Gasping in terror, she reached into her pocket with trembling fingers and pulled her phone out. Had someone discovered her absence already? Sighing in relief, she saw it was a text from Jamila.

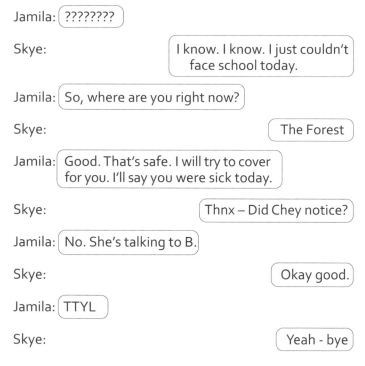

Jamila: ????????

Skye: I know. I know. I just couldn't face school today.

Jamila: So, where are you right now?

Skye: The Forest

Jamila: Good. That's safe. I will try to cover for you. I'll say you were sick today.

Skye: Thnx – Did Chey notice?

Jamila: No. She's talking to B.

Skye: Okay good.

Jamila: TTYL

Skye: Yeah - bye

Skye put her phone back in her pocket and stood looking across the river. The sun danced on the surface of the water as a few pelicans made lazy circles in the sky before coming down to land at the river's edge. In the distance, traffic rumbled and roared as it crossed the bridge leading toward the industrial area of the city. Skye was glad she lived where she did, and she was glad the city had decided to save this little copse of trees and make it into a park. It was aptly named Rubbing Stone Park and the trails crisscrossed through it, most leading to and from the stone. There were benches here and there, inviting people to stop and enjoy the view, and the area and the park were often busy with walkers and joggers and kids out playing. Today, being a school day, it was deserted. That suited Skye just fine.

Ambling along the trails, Skye knew she should feel bad about skipping school, and she did. But mostly she felt like she had been set free. She couldn't say exactly what it was that bothered her about that school. When she actually made a list of things, it didn't seem to add up to much; it didn't seem to be such a big deal. Sage didn't think it was; he just ignored it and got on with things, and so did Miranda. In some ways, Skye wished she could do that too. Whatever it was, it was bothering Chris and Cheyenne too.

Coming back to the rubbing stone, Skye ran her hands along its smooth surface. It had been warmed by the morning sun and it felt good to her touch. Hearing the sound of footsteps nearby, Skye slipped off the path and sat down behind the stone, her back leaning against a tree. A little patch of sunlight beamed through the branches and onto the top of Skye's head. It felt wonderful and Skye closed her eyes, letting her thoughts drift. She had never seen this little cozy, secret place behind the stone before today, even though she spent a lot of time in this park.

Maybe it was the warm sun shining on the top of her head; maybe it was the fact that she hadn't been sleeping all that well for the last few nights; maybe it was the trauma of having skipped school. Whatever it was, the warm sun and cozy spot behind the bison rubbing stone felt safe and secure, and lulled Skye to sleep.

Okômâw came into her dream quickly this time, as if she had something important to tell Skye, but she didn't say anything at all. Okômâw seemed to hover around and above, and it was like she was trying to communicate but the words wouldn't come. Skye wondered, even in her dream, if she just wasn't open enough to hear the message. Was she blocking it somehow?

Okômâw beckoned her to follow and Skye walked along behind her in the dream. Okômâw led Skye to a large expanse of water and they stood on a high hill where the land fell away, giving them a great view of the prairies beyond. Okômâw's lips were moving, but Skye couldn't make out the words; she couldn't hear the sounds and that frustrated her. What was Okômâw trying to tell her?

Then, in Okômâw's hand, Skye saw the beautiful

eagle feather. It was the one she had dreamed about before. It looked like Okômâw was giving her the feather...

Ping!

The sound startled Skye awake and the vision vanished like mist burning off the river. It was her phone, and Skye fumbled it out of her pocket, still half-dazed. She bent over to see the screen, her back and shoulders hunched.

"Oh," she said out loud. "It's from Mom."

Mom: Where are you? You all right? School called me.

Skye: I'm ok. sorry. I'm in The Forest.

Mom: You should be at school!

Skye: I know just didn't feel good.

Mom: Are you sick? Should I come get you?

Skye: No. I'm ok

Mom: Go home and stay there. We'll talk later.

Skye: Ok sorry

Skye sighed. Now she was in trouble, and she'd worried Mom. That wasn't her plan at all. Leaning back, she reached to put her phone into her pocket. Her fingers touched something soft. What was that? Looking down, Skye saw a feather standing up against the buttons on her shirt. It wasn't just any feather; it was the eagle feather from her dreams. Gently, she ran her fingers down its length. It was smooth under her touch, but it almost seemed to sizzle with energy. It tilted sideways across her chest and Skye clasped it firmly to keep it from falling. She knew eagle feathers were sacred to her people and should never touch the ground.

Was this her feather now? She peered around the trees and rubbing stone, almost expecting Okômâw's face to peer back at her. It had been a dream, right? Slowly, Skye made her way back to her house, her mind whirling while her fingers clutched the eagle feather. Okômâw really was trying to tell her something, but what?

Skye pondered that question all day long as she waited for her family to get home. She was restless and paced through the house. TV didn't hold her interest, and neither did trying to read a book or any of the other things she liked to do. Her mind was full of too many questions about Okômâw and the feather. In her room, Skye had placed the feather in a safe but prominent place, on the cork bulletin board over her desk. It was near the dream catcher she had made last year in Culture Club.

After everything else failed, Skye did the only thing she could do around the house; she tidied up. Wouldn't Mom be surprised? She smiled. It wasn't often that Skye volunteered to do extra chores. It wasn't that she was trying to lessen her crime of skipping school, she thought as she unloaded the dishwasher and put the dishes away, the cutlery clattering and chiming as she sorted it into the drawer. It was that she was fidgety and agitated and couldn't settle down. Her mind was too full of questions about her dreams and the eagle feather now hanging in her room.

Stacking the breakfast dishes in the machine, Skye went on to tidy the kitchen and even swept the floor; then she tackled the living room. They weren't a really neat family, as Jamila's was. At Jamila's house, nothing ever seemed to be out of place, but then it was only Jamila, her older brother, Marwan, who was in high school, and their parents.

Skye's house was a rambling bungalow with three bedrooms on the main level. Sage had a bedroom in the basement while Skye, Cheyenne, and their parents all had rooms on the main floor. Large, overstuffed, comfy furniture filled the living room and many large pillows, used when relatives came over, were thrown in the corner near the large TV. Skye had many witsana – relatives – who came and went, dropping by for a meal or to hang out. That was how her family was and she loved it.

Skye loved the pale blue colour of her bedroom

– it reminded her of the sky. The light yellow colour on the ceiling represented the sun, which often peeked in through the window on sunny mornings. Mom and Dad had helped her decorate and paint it a couple of years ago, and Skye had added glow-in-the-dark stars to the ceiling. At night, with the stars on the ceiling shining, Skye felt like she lived and slept among the clouds.

She had a little wooden desk, with two pull-out drawers, which stood against the wall across the room from the bed. Above the desk was a cork bulletin board. On it, Skye pinned special things, like the picture of her and Kôkom and Mósom. In the picture, she was smiling happily into the camera, proudly holding the first fish she had ever caught. There was also a picture of Skye dressed in her favourite regalia – a powder blue and pink dress with white fringes. She felt like a princess in that dress.

Beside the desk, Skye had her own little book-shelf; she loved to read. Books were her favourite Christmas and birthday presents. Skye's dream was to fill that bookshelf with her favourite books and she was well on her way to doing just that!

Skye's phone pinged just as she was finishing tidying her bedroom, dusting the shelves and making her bed. Glancing at the clock on her desk, she saw that school was out. This must be Jamila, she thought, and it was.

Jamila: U ok?

Skye: Fine so far

Jamila: I heard they called your parents

Skye: Yeppers

Jamila: And?????

Skye: Nothing yet until they get home

Jamila: Right. Well keep me posted

Skye: I will

Jamila: xxxx hugs

Skye: Thnx xxxxx

Sage and Cheyenne were the first ones home and they burst in through the front door, yelling Skye's name. "I'm here. I'm here," she said, coming down the hall from her bedroom. "You don't have to yell, you know."

"Skye!" Cheyenne launched herself at Skye, throwing her arms around her waist and squeezing tightly. It was as if she hadn't seen Skye in ages.

"You skipped school!" Sage crowed, dancing around her. "I can't believe it! Miss Goody-Goody skipped school! I thought I'd be the first to do it, but you beat me to it."

Skye glared at him. "It's not funny, you know. I'm going to be in a lot of trouble."

"I'll say," Sage frowned. "The principal came to see me – pulled me out of class to ask about you. It was embarrassing. Some of the kids were laughing at me, saying they knew I'd be a troublemaker."

"Sorry," Skye muttered, but she didn't feel that badly. Sage was really only thinking of himself. Gently prying Cheyenne's arms away, Skye said, "I'm okay, Apisîs. Really. I just needed a break from school today."

Sage looked around the spotless living room. "You did a number on the house. Wow! You think that'll save you from punishment? I doubt it!"

"No, I was just antsy and needed something to do," Skye replied.

"I would have played video games or something," he said. "Cleaning house on a day off from school – you're nuts!"

Skye shrugged, "Maybe." Even though Sage was a pain sometimes, they were really close and she needed his advice. "Actually, I've been having dreams lately."

"Yeah, I know," Sage said, turning to study her. "I heard you telling Mom and Dad."

"What do you dream about?" Cheyenne asked. "Are they scary dreams?"

"No, not really," Skye answered. "There's this old woman – a really old kôkom, I guess. She's been in my dreams ... my visions. She says her name is Okômâw, and I think she's trying to tell me something."

Sage's eyes grew wide. "Wow," he said. "That sounds freaky."

"I know," Skye agreed, feeling Cheyenne's fingers tuck into hers. "Don't be afraid, Cheyenne. Okômâw isn't really scary; it's just confusing. But here's the freaky part..." she turned and walked down the hall, her siblings following closely on her heels.

"What's the freaky part?" Cheyenne pestered, pulling at Skye's clothes. "I want to know."

"I'm going to show you," Skye said, opening her bedroom door and standing back to let the other two proceed into the room. "Notice anything different?"

"Well, it's definitely cleaner," Sage commented as his eyes scanned the room. They came to rest on the bulletin board above her bed. "Hey, where did you get that eagle feather?"

"Yeah," Cheyenne added, skipping across the room and scrambling up on the desk chair to reach it.

"You'll never believe it," Skye murmured, reaching over Cheyenne's head to stroke the feather.

"Well, tell us!" Sage urged. "Last year, I would have killed for a feather like that!"

"But not this year?" Skye turned to look at Sage, assessing him.

"Naw. I got better things to do now."

"Like football?"

"Yeah," Sage said, his voice defensive. "So, tell us about the feather."

Skye took a huge breath and let it out slowly.

"You'll never believe it but, after the school bus took off, I walked to The Forest. You know, Mom was just leaving and I didn't want Dad to see me when he came out, so I walked over to the rubbing stone. I walked around a bit and I got tired, so I laid down and fell asleep. I dreamed again and the old ... Okômâw ... was in my dream and she was trying to tell me something, but I couldn't understand her. Then my phone went off – a text from Jamila. It woke me up and I found the eagle feather."

"On the ground?" Sage questioned, his voice suspicious.

"No," Skye answered, pointed to her shirt. "I was sitting, leaning against the tree and the feather was here – on my chest."

"Wow," both Sage and Cheyenne said together, their voices filled with wonder.

"It's a good thing it didn't touch the dirt," Cheyenne added. Even she knew that eagle feathers were special.

Sage's phone pinged, interrupting the moment, and he read the text. "It's Mom, asking if I'm home and if you're okay."

"Tell her yes," Skye said, backing away from the desk.

Sage continued to read. "She says she and Dad will both be late coming home from work and we need to start supper. She says there's the moose stew in the fridge that we can just warm up."

"Yummy!' Cheyenne said, jumping up and down.

"I love it when Mósom gives us moose meat and Mom makes stew."

"She says there should be some bannock left over too. We should eat before they get home," Sage added as he typed something into his phone. "I told her okay." He looked at Skye as he pocketed his phone. "I guess your punishment is delayed, at least until tomorrow. Mom is taking you to school tomorrow to meet with the principal."

Skye's heart sank, but she nodded, "Yeah, I guess I deserve that." She took Cheyenne by the shoulders and turned her toward the door. "Let's go see about getting supper started. It's going to be a long night," she added under her breath.

"It wouldn't be if you would just try to fit in, you know," Sage admonished. "You have to be more like me. Forget about Culture Club and Powwow Group. Those things don't exist anymore. They're part of the past."

"But why should they be?" Skye retorted, her voice angry. "Isn't school supposed to be a place where we all feel like there's something for all of us there?"

Sage shrugged. "Just choose something else, that's all I'm saying. Try to fit in."

Angry and sad, Skye had no quick comeback for Sage. His easy acceptance of things hurt and confused her.

"But what about the eagle feather?" Cheyenne asked, looking back at it over her shoulder. "What do you think it means?"

"I don't know," Skye murmured. "I just don't know." She was saved from having to answer by another text, again from Jamila.

Jamila | Good news! My mom says to invite your family over tomorrow night for supper. Can you come?

Skye: | I will get Sage to ask and let you know.

"Sage, Jamila is inviting us all over for supper tomorrow. Can you text Mom, since you were already texting her, and ask her?"

"Sure," Sage said easily, reaching for his phone again. The answer pinged back almost immediately. "Mom says great! She will text Jamila's mother to see what we can bring. She sounds like she's in a happier mood now," he added. Skye was relieved. She didn't like being in trouble.

"Hmm," Cheyenne said, licking her lips. "I love Jamila's mom's cooking! I hope she makes those stuffed potato things – yummy! Those keb ... keb..." she paused. "I forget how to say it, but they're delicious!"

"Yes!" Skye agreed. She loved the fried potato skins stuffed with onions, pumpkin and sometimes raisins. "I think they're called kebbe heeleh," she said, trying to remember.

"I love the shish barak," Sage declared, rubbing

his stomach. "All those little meat balls cooked in that yummy sauce. I can't wait till tomorrow!"

The moose stew was forgotten, at least for a while, Skye thought in amusement. But she knew they would enjoy it soon, even while thinking of all the Lebanese food they would eat tomorrow night. However, first, Skye would have to talk to Mom and Dad tonight, and tomorrow she would have to go see Mrs. Miller. The anxiety of it all almost ruined her appetite.

Chapter Five

"Good morning," Mrs. Miller said briskly the next morning. She looked sternly at Skye, her lips pursed together in a long, thin line. "I see we have some problems to discuss." She escorted Skye and Mom into her office, where she moved around behind her desk and sat down. "Take those chairs," she pointed to two chairs on the other side of her wide desk.

Skye's mother raised her eyebrows at Skye and squeezed her hand reassuringly as they walked toward the large desk. Skye knew that signal. She had seen her mother stand up to other people whom she felt were trying to get the better of her. She watched as Mom straightened her shoulders. "I didn't catch your name," Skye's mother said pointedly, even though she knew who the principal was. She stood and reached a hand across the wide desk. "My name is Wâpan Bird."

"Ohh," Mrs. Miller said, awkwardly fumbling to stand. She put three fingers into Wâpan's hand for a brief moment, then sat down, quickly shuffling the papers in front of her. Skye had heard the expression "limp handshake" before; now she knew what it meant. It was like Mrs. Miller didn't like to shake hands or didn't want to shake her mother's hand. "It states here that your name is Dawn."

"Yes, my English name is Dawn, but in the past couple of years our family has been exploring more of our cultural and historical roots – getting back to our roots, so to speak – and we are going back to our Cree names. 'Wâpan' means 'dawn' in Cree."

"Well, Wa-wa... Mrs. Bird," the principal struggled. "We seem to have a problem with Skye. She's just not fitting in."

Mom squeezed Skye's fingers tightly and Skye knew Mom was trying to hold on to her temper. "It's not a problem with Skye," she said softly, although Skye could hear a thread of steel in her voice and was glad Mom was on her side. "What is the school doing to accommodate the transition of the students into this new situation?"

"Ahhhh," Mrs. Miller stammered lamely. "Well, everyone else seems to be fitting in just fine," she finally spit out.

"You think they are," Mom said, "but my guess is that if Skye is struggling, others are as well."

"We are not here to discuss other students, Mrs. Bird." The principal's voice was full of authority. "We are here to discuss why Skye skipped school yesterday. We can't have students missing school. We don't know where they are and it sets a bad example for the rest of the student body. They will all begin to think that they can miss school just because they don't feel like going."

"I skipped school because I don't like it here," Skye interrupted.

"But you have made no effort to fit in, Skye," Mrs. Miller retorted. "No wonder you don't like it. You haven't joined any clubs or activity groups, and you haven't even attempted to make friends."

"I would join Culture Club, Powwow Group, or something like that," Skye offered. "I just don't see anything on the list I want to belong to."

"Then perhaps you are not trying hard enough." Mrs. Miller looked down her nose at Skye.

"Can't you start a Powwow Group here, or a Culture Club? I'm sure Skye would help lead it; she has a lot of good ideas and a lot of experience," Mom suggested.

Mrs. Miller sighed. "We just don't have the personnel to run extra groups, and we don't have anyone with experience in these areas."

"I'm sure a Culture Club would be easy enough to start," Mom replied patiently. "Everyone under-stands their own culture and has something to share." She thought for a moment. "Did any of the teachers or other staff transfer from the old school to this one?" she asked.

"As you may recall," Mrs. Miller talked to Mom as if Mom didn't remember anything at all, "the students from the old school were divided into three groups and transferred over from the city's centre to three newer schools in the suburbs. This school received the smallest number of students and, therefore, the smallest number of staff transferred over. We have two educational assistants who work in the younger classes."

Mom glanced at Skye and Skye could see Mom restraining herself from rolling her eyes. "That's unbelievable. As parents, we were led to believe that our children would see and be able to talk to staff from their former school."

"Well," Mrs. Miller sniffed, "I suppose that's true enough if you go to one of the other schools, but here, we only got the two staff members, as I already mentioned."

"Still," Mom persisted, "a Culture Club would be a positive step for our children – for all the children and staff at this school."

Mrs. Miller dismissed this idea with the wave of a hand. "I'm afraid Skye will have to find something else to join.

"Now," she changed the subject, "about Skye missing school."

Seeing that this meeting was getting nowhere, Skye jumped in. "I promise I won't skip school again, Mrs. Miller."

"Good. That's very good." Mrs. Miller rose to her feet, her hands spread wide on the desk. "Well, thank you for coming in, Mrs. Bird. I'm sure we won't have any more trouble with Skye." The phone sitting on the desk jingled and Mrs. Miller practically dove for it, effectively ending the meeting.

"Come on, Skye," her mother said, putting an arm around her shoulders. "Walk me to the car."

Once outside the school, Skye's mom expelled a lungful of pent-up air and frustration. "Oh my goodness!" she fumed. "Now I see what you're up against." She pulled Skye into a bear hug. "I'm so sorry, My Girl. That was a terrible meeting. That principal doesn't seem to be concerned with you at all, but only with making sure the other students don't follow your example of skipping school."

"I know," Skye said. "I'm sorry I caused trouble, Mom. I will try to fit in."

"That's not really the problem or the answer here," Mom sighed. "There are bigger things going on and I'm not sure how to address them. Especially since she doesn't even see them. Let's just think about this for a while, okay? I think we need to talk to Dad and Kôkom and Mósom and other elders too."

Skye nodded. She knew Mom wasn't trying to avoid the situation; she just had a lot of things going on in her life. Besides, it was a good idea to get advice from her grandparents. "Okay," she agreed.

They said their goodbyes and Skye watched her mom get into their car and drive away. Then she walked reluctantly back into the school and down the hall to Mrs. Bone's class. As she neared the classroom door, she spied Justin and Raven sitting on the floor near the door. "What's going on?" she asked.

"Got kicked outta class," Justin laughed, shrugging his shoulders. "Talking too much, I guess."

"I guess," Raven sighed. "My Mom's not gonna be happy with me. She doesn't want to come into the school to have to deal with anything, you know. And you got me in trouble — again!" She punched Justin hard on the arm.

"Sorry," Justin muttered. "I didn't mean to; it's just so boring in there." He turned his gaze to Skye. "What do you think?"

"Yeah, it's boring," Skye agreed, wishing she could defend Mrs. Bone. She didn't like dissing teachers.

"I don't know why we had to come to this dumb school, anyway," Raven groused, twirling a strand of her long, dark hair around her finger. "I don't feel like we do anything!"

"Nothing fun, anyway," Justin agreed. He scratched his head, "I mean, I don't feel like we learn anything either."

The door opened abruptly and Mrs. Bone stepped into the hallway. "Come with me, you two," she said, pointing to Raven and Justin.

"Where are we going?" Raven asked, getting reluctantly to her feet.

"To Mrs. Miller's office," came the dark reply.

"For speaking out in class?" Skye burst out.

"That's not so bad, really," she tried to defend her classmates.

Raven and Justin gave her quick little smiles of thanks.

"Quiet, Miss Skye, or you will join them as well," Mrs. Bone declared. "I will not put up with misbehaviour in my class! Now, to the principal's office!"

"Wow," Justin muttered under his breath, "just for talking. It feels like corporal punishment around here."

"Yeah," Raven spoke. "I don't see the other kids getting in trouble so much, and they talk all the time."

"That's not true!" Mrs. Bone spoke sternly. The noises coming from the classroom proved otherwise, but she chose to ignore them. "You are being disrespectful! Now get moving!"

Skye watched as Justin and Raven followed Mrs. Bone down the hallway toward the office, laughter and silliness coming from her classroom. It didn't feel fair somehow that only two got into trouble – and two new kids – when everyone else was misbehaving as well. Sighing at the injustice, she walked back into the classroom as a paper airplane swooped past her head. It didn't seem fair at all. Ignoring the noise and other goings-on in the room, Skye buried herself in her novel, blocking out the sounds – which got louder and louder. Looking around, she caught Tyrell's silent gaze across the room. "Talk to you at recess," he mouthed, and

Skye nodded, wondering what he wanted. Tyrell was the strong, silent type who rarely said anything.

At recess, Justin and Raven were still sitting outside the front office as Tyrell and Skye walked by. "You okay?" Skye asked, stopping in front of them.

Raven shrugged. "She's calling our parents and we have to have a meeting."

"Yeah," Justin muttered, "just for talking – whispering actually. It wasn't much, or about anything important either. It sure seems like it's the new kids that are getting in trouble in that classroom."

Mrs. Miller chose that moment to come out of her office. "It does seem like the new students are having trouble adjusting," she stated, her hands on her hips. "We have been most welcoming and accommodating to you, and you all are not showing any respect or consideration."

"I wonder why that is," Tyrell muttered, bowing his head so that his long, dark hair fell across his forehead, shielding his eyes.

"Do you know something I don't know, Mr. LaVallee?" Mrs. Miller asked a question but, to Skye, it sounded more like a threat .

Tyrell was silent for a moment; then he raised his head and looked directly into her eyes. "Here's what I see," he said, pointing to his own chest. "I see the new kids getting in trouble, and who are the new kids?" he asked. When nobody responded, he continued, "It's the kids with the coloured skin; that's who always seems to be sitting here outside this office. I don't see too many other kids sitting here, do you?"

"Well," Mrs. Miller blustered, "that's who seems to need all the guidance and help adjusting here. Those are the students not following the rules."

"Is that so?" Tyrell asked, jamming his baseball cap over his head. "Or are we just the ones that get pointed out – taken down?" Turning, he stalked out of the school, leaving Mrs. Miller sputtering.

Skye followed Tyrell out into the blustery morning. "You're right," she said, coming to stand beside him.

"I know I am, but what can we do about it?"

"I don't know," Skye said. "I just don't know..."

That night, the eagle feather almost glowed in the glare of the streetlight shining through Skye's bedroom window. It was "silly o'clock in the morning", as Cheyenne liked to say when she woke up in the middle of the night. Peering at the clock on the nightstand, Skye could see that it was approaching three o'clock in the morning – it was silly o'clock, and she hadn't fallen asleep yet.

Tossing and turning, she had tried to calm her mind and turn her thoughts off, but nothing was working. All she could think of was that awful meeting she and Mom had that morning, and how nothing had been resolved. School was still a difficult place for Skye and she didn't know how to make herself fit in. That would be the easiest thing, really, if she could just switch off her feelings like Sage did and learn to fit in with everyone else and not complain about things.

Sighing, Skye tossed off the blankets and got out of bed, the large T-shirt she wore falling to her knees. It was a hand-me-down from Dad, and her favourite nighttime attire. It had been washed so many times that it was soft and comfy. She felt the material brush against the backs of her legs as she walked across the dark room, lighted only by the streetlight and the soft green glow of the clock. The light played upon the eagle feather, making it gleam, and Skye pulled it off the bulletin board, holding it tightly to her chest, her fingers tingling with electricity.

Skye thought she could hear the sound of a drum beating in the distance; the ancient sound of her people filling her senses. It engulfed her soul and she closed her eyes, clutching the feather to her chest. Suddenly, the drum became her heartbeat. It beat louder and louder as she felt the vibrations against her skin, her cheeks, her eyes, and she knew she was living and breathing the sound.

Holding the feather high, Skye felt something electrical flow through her body.

It was like magic. Then she was spinning. She

twirled and twirled until she felt the whole world spinning with her...

Everything seemed to blur and, somehow, Skye slipped back in time.

Chapter Six

How long Skye stood stone-still like a statue, her eyes closed, she didn't know. Was it one minute? Two minutes? A day? A lifetime?

The first sign that things were very different was the feel of the floor against her feet. It was softer, and tilted! She must be dizzy from all the twirling, she thought as she sank to her knees. A warm breeze caressed her cheeks. Where that was coming from? she wondered. Then she smelled smoke. It reminded her of a campfire – a big log bonfire like they sometimes had at the lake.

Slowly, Skye opened her eyes. Glancing around, she could see ... nothing.

Nothing but the long prairie grass waving in the soft breeze. And a winding river far below, and hills – some steep, some gently rolling – down to the water's edge. And the bright sun hovering on the distant horizon.

Skye realized she was sitting beside a boulder, halfway up a steep hill. A few bushes grew around the boulder, sheltering her from sight. About 100 metres above her, the land seemed to level off, like the prairie she was used to seeing.

Gasping in great surprise, her heart pounding wildly in her chest, Skye tried to take everything in at once. Where was she? She should be safely at home, in her bedroom. What on earth had happened to her?

She felt her heart thumping in her throat as she tried to piece together this strange new world. Scared but curious, she continued to look around. "What's going on?" Skye called out, trying to catch her breath. "Where am I?"

"You are on a journey, Awâsis," Okômâw said as she suddenly appeared behind her. "It is a journey of knowledge and learning."

"Oh my goodness!" Skye burst out, startled but happy to see Okômâw and to have someone to talk to – someone she kind of knew, even if it was only through her dreams.

Okômâw smiled. "It is time, My Child. It is only now that you are ready to listen, to hear, and to learn."

"Where am I?" Skye demanded, looking around at her panoramic view from this spot on the edge of the high hill.

"I will let you figure that out, Awâsis," Okômâw said. "That is part of the journey as well."

Cautiously, so scared she was shaking, Skye peered around. She could hear the sound of drums beating in the distance. The smell of campfire smoke drifted toward her and she could smell meat cooking. Squeezing her eyes tightly closed, Skye shook her head from side to side, as if to clear it. She willed things to change back to what she was used to. She willed herself back to her warm, safe bedroom.

"You are on this journey for now," Okômâw informed her, "You have nothing to fear, for you are merely an observer of a past time in our history. You will not be able to interfere or communicate with humans. You should watch and learn from the past, to gather strength and to know what you need to do in your present life. When you have learned something, I will reappear." Slowly, before Skye's eyes, Okômâw disappeared like smoke on a winter's breeze, and Skye found herself completely alone; but she wasn't really afraid anymore.

Gazing around, Skye wondered what her lesson would be.

Down the hill, the land levelled off and she spied many small tents dotting the ground. She smiled when she realized that they weren't tents – they were tipis! Automatically, Skye began to count them but soon lost track. She could see what looked to be hundreds of them. It looked like a whole city made up of tipis.

A movement caught her eye at the top of the hill. Something was moving slowly on the land above her. Skye hung onto a nearby bush for balance and then, taking a few steps, she extended her neck and gazed upward toward the movement.

Bison! Thousands of bison stretched out as far as the eye could see. They looked like one massive piece of melted chocolate spreading out over the land. There were so many bison that the whole area was brown! All of the creatures were shaggy and dark brown, but the babies were a lighter colour, and there sure seemed to be a lot of them, prancing and running around the large herd.

As Skye watched, a curious calf came closer to the edge of the cliff. One brown eye peered down at Skye. "You're so cute!" Skye exclaimed. The little one seemed to smile at her, its long pink tongue reaching down to snag a few blades of grass that hung over the edge of the cliff. "Be careful," Skye warned. "You don't want to fall; it's a long way down."

On the top of the calf's head, Skye could see two small white bumps just becoming visible on its head. She realized that someday, when the calf grew up, these would be horns. All bison – male and female – had horns.

Suddenly a loud, angry snort filled the air and Skye jumped. A massive, curly brown head swung over the edge and peered down at her. It had huge, pointy horns and scary eyes. A low, rumbled threat growled out of its throat and Skye thought the hairy beast might jump over the cliff and come after her!

She scrambled back into the bushes to hide. Holding her breath, Skye watched as the big bison gazed down for a couple of seconds, then swung its big head at the younger one. They both disappeared from view and Skye breathed a sigh of relief. Thank goodness they were going to leave her alone! Skye figured that must have been the mother bison, concerned for her baby.

Skye stood up and watched as the mother and calf joined the rest of the other bison grazing peacefully at the top of the rise. Then she became aware, once again, of the drumming sound echoing up from the river valley below.

Where were all the people? With so many tipis around, there had to be people too. Her eyes followed the sound of the drums. Just past the tipis, on a large, flat area beside the river, the people had gathered. Many were dancing, bouncing around in a great, crowded mass. Others were sitting in groups on the sidelines, watching. There must be hundreds of people gathered together in this sheltered valley beside the river.

Suddenly the sound of the drums vibrating through the air became more intense. Every beat seemed to call her name. The drumbeat beckoned. It soothed her and calmed her down. It was a connection. Past to present, the music was still the same, and it drew her toward the people. Slowly, Skye made her way out of the bushes. Brushing at her clothes, she found that she was wearing a simple dress made of tanned fabric she surmised was deer hide. It felt soft to the touch.

Thin leather fringes draped down her like sleeves and tickled her arms when she moved. Pretty white shells and fluffy white feathers had been tied to the ends of the fringes and were fastened onto the front of the dress in simple patterns. The dress was long, reaching almost to her ankles. Her moccasins looked to be made of one piece of hide that wrapped around each foot and was tied with a thin leather strip. They were also decorated with feathers and a few beads. Around her waist was tied a thin strip of leather used for a belt. It didn't look like any dress or regalia she had ever seen.

Spying a well-worn path leading down the gentlest part of the slope, Skye ventured forward. Tentatively at first, she followed the path as the drums continued to beat in the distance. With each step, the drumbeats became louder and more distinct. They seemed to be welcoming her.

The sun, hovering just over the western horizon, cast long shadows across the land. Skye guessed that it would soon be dark. Walking carefully, she made her way down the hill and right into the first campsite. Pausing behind the first tipi she came to, Skye surveyed the area, searching for people. No one walked between the tipis. No one was tending the slow-burning campfires. No one sat on the thick, bison rugs set out in front of each tipi. They were all at the big powwow.

Suddenly, something cool and wet touched her fingers. Skye jumped and yelped in surprise, then quickly covered her mouth to keep the sound trapped inside. Looking down, she saw a medium-sized dog standing beside her. "N-nice doggie," Skye stammered and wondered in surprise that the dog could see her! She reached shaky fingers out to touch the top of its brown head. A warm tongue licked at her fingers and Skye relaxed. The dog seemed friendly enough. It wagged its tail a few times and then plopped down on the bison rug in front of the tipi.

Searching the shadows created by the setting sun and the tipis, Skye realized that at almost every tipi doorway, a dog was lounging nearby. Skye hoped they were all as friendly and relaxed as this one. Standing statue-still, Skye watched the dogs as they watched her. They didn't seem to feel the need to protect the tipis and, slowly, they closed their eyes and buried their heads on their paws. Skye breathed a sigh of relief. All of the dogs were ignoring her and that was a good thing!

Cautiously, walking silently in her moccasins, Skye moved among the tipis, her fingers stretching out to touch the soft tanned hides. It was like a little village,

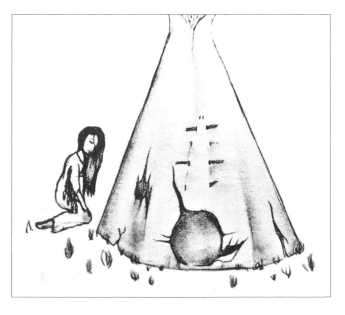

she thought, turning in a complete circle as she surveyed the tidy homes. The people – real people – her people – lived and slept here.

One tipi was brighter than the others. Its sides were painted with coloured symbols and designs faded by the sun. Beside the tipi, two straight branches had been pounded into the ground. They looked like the letter 'y'. In the vee of these branches, another strong branch had been laid. Across this branch, pieces of red meat had been hung. Skye wondered if they were being smoked and dried.

Stepping silently past the tipi, Skye came to a large wooden rack. Stretched across it was the biggest piece of bison hide she had ever seen; the hide and meat drying on the racks were bison. She must be at a bison hunt. Skye remembered that whenever the people killed the bison, they gave thanks with music, songs and dance. That's probably what they were doing right now, giving thanks for all the bison meat and skins they had. Looking back at the high, steep hill she had just walked down, Skye made another connection. That looked exactly like the bison jumps she had seen in books and at the local interpretive centre.

A group of tired travellers arrived, with dogs hitched to stick-like contraptions Skye recalled were travois. They had pulled them across the prairies. Each travois consisted of long poles made from trees. On each were strapped food, goods and the material to set up a tipi. Skye watched as the travellers were greeted, offered food and water, and welcomed into the ever-growing group.

Skye gazed around, taking in the spectacular sight along the river's edge and beyond. Now she really understood. This was what it was like for her people thousands of years ago; before the Europeans came. Her people had been very successful hunters. They knew how to prepare the meat and the hides. They had thrived and been a strong and proud people. Skye felt her heart glow with warmth and pride.

Then the earth began to shimmer and shake; the sound of the drums became more intense. "You have learned well, Awâsis." Skye heard Okômâw's voice and felt her warm touch as the world spun away and left her spiralling in space.

Skye felt her mind begin to whirl. Lights flashed behind her eyelids and she heard the far-off sound of drums. She twirled faster and faster until everything became one big blur of noise and light. Then slowly, the world righted itself and Skye opened her eyes and looked around. Okômâw was right behind her, her eyes filled with sadness. But a sense of excitement spread through Skye's limbs.

"I recognize it!" she cried, peering down toward the trees. "Look! There's the small village of tipis!

There's the river! This is it! This is the same place we just left!" Skye swivelled her head in every direction at once, trying to take everything in. "Something is missing..."

Stretching her neck, she looked up the hill, knowing what she would see. "Wait a minute," she muttered, scanning the empty land. "Where are all the bison, and what's all that white stuff up there?" On the hills overlooking the river valley, white mounds that looked like small white branches and bigger white rocks dotted the area. They looked like big piles of white marshmallows glistening in the sun. There almost seemed to be as many of those as there had been bison. "Whatever that is, there's sure a lot of it," she muttered.

Then she heard a rumbling sound that snorted and hissed a short distance away. "That sounds like a ... like a ... train," Skye finished as it rattled into view, clicking and clacking along on the long ribbon of rail she could see stretching across the empty prairie.

Skye stared at the white mounds again, then looked toward the sound of the train as it rumbled across the grassland. She thought about the history book she had been reading. A funny, queasy feeling began to grow in the pit of her stomach. She glanced back at Okômâw. "Go and find out, Awâsis," she said. "This is another part of your journey." Okômâw looked as if she was going to say more, then she slowly shook her head and Skye could feel her acute sadness. "Go, Awâsis. This part you must know as well. Even though it will pain you greatly." Nodding, Skye watched as Okômâw disappeared on a puff of smoke.

Heading down the steep slope toward the tiny village, Skye had a feeling she already knew what those white piles were. And why were there so few tipis here now? Where was everyone?

A forlorn drum beat slowly in the distance. It was only one drum, and it sounded sad. Skye knew something was wrong and she hurried down the hill toward the tipis. They were set up in a circle, just like before, but they looked different somehow. The hides used to cover the tipi poles were very worn and frayed. In places, pieces of hide flapped in the brisk breeze, exposing the inside of the tipis to the wind and rain. That didn't look good at all.

Pressing her fingers to her lips, Skye took a few steps into the village. There were a few people about, but they hurried from one tipi to another, their heads down. The clothes the people wore were tattered and torn and worn to rags. Some people reclined on buffalo rugs in front of the tipis and they seemed to be too sick and weak to move. There were a few dogs too, but they were mangy and skinny, their ribs almost sticking out of their chests. They looked half-starved.

A frail-looking older man stumbled out of the tipi closest to Skye. Bleary-eyed from fever, he seemed to see her. "Help me," he cried weakly as he stumbled past her and into the arms of a man dressed in a long, flowing black robe. He had a funny-looking hat on his head and a long necklace of heavy beads with a cross at the end of it.

"We have no food," the old man cried, gesturing weakly toward the vast prairie. "The buffalo – our food – is gone. There is not one buffalo left here, and the other animals have been trapped and eaten. We have no way to mend our tipis." He pointed to all of the ripped tipi covers. "We have no clothes to keep us warm; no furs." Touching his worn leather dress, he stumbled as he held up one foot. His left moccasin was ragged and almost falling off his foot.

The old man continued to speak, as if in a trance: "It has happened as the wise men and elders predicted. Many, many white-skinned people came from across the big water – as many as there are fish in the river, and they are still coming. The white leaders encouraged the slaughter of the buffalo to weaken us, so that we would surrender. The people have settled on our land. They put a long line of steel trees down on the ground and then the big iron horses came, snorting smoke and fire. The remaining buffalo got killed because they were in the way. Our way of life is vanishing." The old man looked pale and stricken. Gulping for air, he grasped his chest as if it hurt. Coughing once, he continued:

"We were once strong and mighty. We numbered many; too many to count – like the mighty buffalo.

Now – like the buffalo – we are few," he said sadly. "Some have died of strange sicknesses, some died of the cold, and the rest of us will die of hunger soon. The hunters who are able go out looking for food, but they have not been rewarded for their efforts. The animals are gone, both small and large. We have heard that there is food at the forts the white-skinned people have built. If we can only get our strength up, we can walk to the fort." The old man's words faded away like wisps of dandelion fluff blowing in the wind.

Skye watched as the man in black – a priest, she figured out – took the old man to another tipi and helped him inside.

"I am so sad," Skye murmured, looking around at the devastation. Her eyes filled with tears and rolled, unheeded, down her cheeks. "My people were strong and healthy, but now they are weak and dying. They are suffering. Everything has changed for them: the bison are gone, left as white piles of bones in the grass; and sickness and diseases are attacking them. My heart bleeds for my people." Skye dropped to her knees in the dirt and sobbed.

Chapter Seven

Skye awoke in her bed at dawn, clutching the eagle feather to her chest, her face stiff with dried tears. What had happened? Was it all just a bad dream? But it seemed so vivid; so real that she could almost reach out and touch the remnants of the torn and ripped tipis she had seen. Her heart felt like it was broken in two and tears gathered in her eyes again as she thought of the horrible conditions her people had had to survive. Pushing off the covers, she got out of bed and found that she was wearing her oversized T-shirt. Her knees felt sore and she stooped to rub them. Little bits of dirt and gravel came away and bounced onto the carpet. "What?" Skye said aloud as she sank back onto the bed. So it wasn't a dream?

A loud banging sounded on her bedroom door and Skye jumped. "Mom says it's time to get up," Cheyenne yelled.

"Okay, okay," Skye called back, trying to clear her head.

"She said to hurry or you'll be late. She doesn't want you to miss the bus."

"Okay," Skye mumbled again. "I'm coming." Pushing her thoughts away, she rehung the eagle feather in its place on the bulletin board and went to get dressed. She had a lot to think about.

On the bus ride to school, Skye tried to explain to Jamila what had happened, but all the words rushed out, jumbled and confusing. "So, you're having these weird dreams with an old lady in them?" Jamila summed up, frowning. "And you feel like you're going back in time in your dreams?"

"No," Skye said. "I AM going back in time!" She lifted her knees. "See these?" She pointed to little indents in both knees. "I dreamed I was kneeling on gravel and dirt last night, and I was!"

Jamila was silent, not knowing what to say. She gently fingered the little holes in Skye's knees. "Wow, that's cool. I'd like to go back in time too."

"Yeah, it was really cool, now that I think about it," Skye admitted. "At least the first time period I went to. I mean, I saw thousands of bison grazing on the prairies, and I saw so many of my people – the Cree! And they were happy and healthy and proud. That was the period of time called 'pre-contact', you know – before all the Europeans came to this land. It was amazing to see that. But then..."

Skye's face turned sad and her eyes filled with gloom. "Then came the time afterward. It was so terrible to see. The people – my people – were starving. There was nothing left to eat. They were sick, too, from diseases the Europeans carried with them." She sighed. "I'd like to learn more about that. You know, like what kinds of diseases did they bring? How many people died? What was it really like here before the Europeans came?"

"Maybe you could do an inquiry project about it," Jamila offered, "I mean, it's a great topic. I'm doing one right now in my class."

"You are?" Skye frowned. "I'll ask Mrs. Bone. Maybe we could do an inquiry project like your class. That would be fun." The bus lurched to a stop and the girls disembarked with the rest of the students.

After attendance was called and students were setting up to work on reading on the mini laptops, powering up the tiny things and logging in, Skye got brave and raised her hand. "Yes, Skye," Mrs. Bone frowned. "Don't ask to be excused to use the washrooms; it's too early for that."

"N-no," Skye murmured, "that's not it. I'm just wondering if we're going to be doing inquiry projects in class this year. I mean, I enjoy them so much and they seem like such a great way to learn!

I love hearing what everyone else is doing and I learn so much when we all share our work—"

"I see," Mrs. Bone interrupted as some of the other students snickered at Skye.

"Nerd," Calvin called from the back of the classroom. Everyone laughed.

"Enough, everyone," Mrs. Bone said firmly. "Yes, we will be doing science projects. I will give you a list of topics this afternoon."

"B-but..." Skye stammered. Part of the fun of inquiry projects was getting to choose your own topic – something you were super interested in. Skye knew sometimes the teacher selected topics ahead of time, but the best projects were when kids got to choose their own topics.

"Never mind that now," Mrs. Bone said firmly, ending all talk of inquiry projects. "We will discuss it this afternoon."

True to her word, when the students came in from afternoon recess, there was a long list of animal names on the board. "Now settle down," Mrs. Bone said as the students found their seats. "We will be doing a research project, as Skye mentioned. I have selected several animals I thought might be of interest to you. Now, I want you to read the list and choose two or three you would be interested in doing.

"I'm going to call your name and ask you to tell me which animal you want to research. Remember, if someone else has already spoken for that animal, you can't choose it. I have put six or seven extra animals on the board, so you will get some choice; even the person choosing last." The class moaned. It was inevitable that someone would really want to choose an animal already chosen and would be left researching one they really weren't interested in.

"I'm going to start with Skye," Mrs. Bone announced, smiling at Skye, dry-erase marker poised near the list. "Since you seem so eager, I wanted to reward you by letting you have first choice."

Skye scanned the list on the board. There were exotic animals like giraffe, elephant, tiger and leopard. There were ocean animals like various species of whales, dolphins and even octopi and stingray. There were insects, amphibians and reptiles, but what Skye couldn't find was any animal that really interested her. "What about the bison?" she asked tentatively. "I'd really like to learn something about the bison." She stammered and went silent, but thoughts of her time with Okômâw last night flooded her brain. She felt something akin to bravery blossom like an awakening inside her. "I mean, after all," she said more loudly, "the bison once roamed all over this land." She waved her arm toward the window and several students looked outside as if hoping to see a bison stroll past.

Mrs. Bone sighed loudly and laid the marker down to fold her arms tightly over her chest. "Are you deliberately trying to be difficult, Skye?"

Hurt to the core, as the students giggled and laughed around her, Skye felt her face flush scarlet. Heat pulsed around her eyes. She looked at the board quickly. "Jellyfish," she whispered, bravery vanishing inside her like a deflated balloon. Her only thought was to get Mrs. Bone to quit looking at her like that. "I will research the jellyfish."

Mrs. Bone wrote her name beside the animal and moved on to Jesse. Skye breathed a sigh of relief, glad the students were listening and watching the teacher, hoping to get the animal of their choice. They had forgotten about Skye.

But Skye hadn't forgotten what happened. Her face still burned with embarrassment and she kept her head down, pretending to doodle on a page of her notebook. Why had Mrs. Bone been so mean to her? She was only asking a simple question.

After the lengthy process of choosing animals, Mrs. Bone took them all to the library to choose books. "Baby," Miranda whispered and poked Skye in the back as she walked past with two of her new friends. "Why must you be so difficult, Skye?" she mimicked and the other girls burst into giggles.

"Get lost, Miranda," Skye forced words through her clenched teeth and turned away, listening as the librarian told students where they could find the books they needed for their projects. The students rushed between two aisles where most of the animal books were shelved, leaving Skye alone.

Another student lingered nearby, running his

finger over the row of books in front of him, his blond curls falling over his forehead, and she remembered that his name was Jack. He looked up at her as she tried to squeeze around him. "Hi," he said, his blue eyes twinkling. "Care to do research on jellyfish with me?" he laughed.

At first Skye thought he was making fun of her, then she realized that he was sympathizing with her. "I have to do the California condor," he said, shaking his head. "It's an okay bird, but I'm not really interested. I'd rather research the govern-mental policies of Canada during World War II."

Skye couldn't help herself; she laughed. "Really? That's what you're interested in?"

Jack shrugged his shoulders. "Yes, actually. The war really affected my great-grandparents, since my great-grandfather came home wounded and they had to amputate his right leg. I'd like to under-stand all that stuff.

"To each their own," Skye murmured.

"Exactly!" Jack smiled. "Now I'm stuck learning about a bird that doesn't even live around here on the prairies when I'd rather do my own research on my own topic.

"At least you tried to change her mind; good for you, Skye." He patted her awkwardly on the shoulder, then turned back to the shelf, continuing to hunt for suitable books.

Not wanting to be amongst the crowd of kids right now, Skye thought about her other project –

the real research project she wanted to do. She walked toward the history section in the library, smiling. Maybe she and Jack could be friends. He seemed like a nice kid – in a weird sort of way.

The dismissal bell rang and Skye exited the library without any resources. She would have to go to the public library again to find books for both her projects. She wondered if she would be able to go tonight. She wasn't excited about jellyfish, but she was burning with desire to know more about the Indigenous peoples who had lived hundreds and thousands of years ago. That's the research she was eager to start.

Hurrying to Cheyenne's classroom, she caught up with her as she was leaving the classroom door, backpack in hand. "I'm going to text Mom quickly to see if we can walk to the public library," she said, pulling out her phone.

"Better text Dad, I think," Cheyenne said, struggling with her backpack. "Remember, Mom said she was going to be super busy today at work."

"Oh yeah," Skye muttered as she began to punch letters into the phone.

Skye:

> Hey Dad, can Chey and I walk to the public library and not go home on the bus today?

Dad:

> Sure, but stay there. I'll come get you. I need a few books too. Let Sage know, and remember, we're having supper at the Hajjar's house tonight.

Skye: Ok, thnx. I did forget.

Dad: Love you, My Girl.

Skye: Love you 2

"We need to catch Sage quickly," Skye said, shoving her phone into her back pocket and grabbing Cheyenne's hand. Together, they hurried from the school to find Sage and to let the bus driver know they wouldn't be on the bus that day.

Later at the library, Skye helped Cheyenne find a few books, then found her own. They settled into the window seat overlooking the street and opened their books. Skye had two books about jellyfish stacked at the bottom of her pile; she'd read those later. In her hands, she leafed through a book about life in North America before the Europeans arrived. It showed many examples of a thriving life for the Indigenous people. There were many, many groups and people spread all over Canada and the United States, and there were also many groups flourishing in Central and South America. The book showed how the peoples were inventive, altering their own environment to suit their needs, and purposefully breeding plants, such as corn or maize, to alter their genetics, and make edible food products. The indigenous peoples of Mexico figured out how to alter plants to make maize. Her own people, The Cree, used plants for medicinal purposes and made dyes out of berries.

The book was called *Before Columbus*. Skye loved the title. It contained the kind of information she wanted to learn, she thought as she continued to flip the pages until she came to details about diseases and how they had killed so many Indigenous people. Skye thought about her time with Okômâw and remembered the sickness she had seen in the night. It broke her heart to think that so many people got sick and died. She wanted to know why. This book would help her understand, and wouldn't Okômâw be proud of her? Skye had to smile at that, and it felt good. This was where she would start to read!

When Dad came into the children's section of the library, both Cheyenne and Skye were totally engaged in their reading. Skye didn't hear Dad until Cheyenne said, "Oh, hi, Dad."

Dad smiled and mussed Cheyenne's hair. "You were both so busy reading, I hated to interrupt you. Still having trouble finding books in your school library?" he asked, noticing the book Skye had in her hands.

Skye nodded. "This is a great book, Dad; have you seen it?"

Dad picked up the book and examined it, reading the cover and noting the author's name. "Oh, no.

I haven't read this book, but the author has written an adult book on the same topic. I think this is his kid's version. I love that he's making this information accessible to kids by having great pictures, maps and charts. I'd like to read it when you're finished with it, if you don't mind. I'm sure I can learn something too."

"Sure!" Skye agreed, eager to share her new knowledge. "It says here that the Europeans were immune to diseases like smallpox; they might get sick, but they had a greater chance of surviving the illness. But our people had no immunity and died by the thousands. There's also information about pigs being brought over for food by the explorers. Did you know pigs carry diseases?" Skye was practically shouting with excitement. "The explorers just let the pigs go loose and, mostly, they followed the men, but they wandered off too. They infected our people with things like tuberculous and anthrax, and they infected the wild animals like turkeys and deer. It's so sad to think that so many people died from something so simple. I love this book!" Skye hugged it to her chest.

"You are a wealth of knowledge," Dad laughed, pulling Skye to her feet. "I'm glad you're reading this," he added, his eyes serious. "Information is power and the more you know about the collective history of our Peoples, the better."

Skye smiled. "I know, Dad. You're always telling us that."

"Okay, okay. Come on, you two," Dad smiled, helping the girls gather up their books. "We need to go home. You can tell me more about this book on the way to Jamila's house."

Mom and Sage met them at the Hajjar residence. Good smells were already filling the house when Jamila opened the door to Skye, Cheyenne and Dad. "Yum!" Cheyenne sniffed the air, rubbing her stomach. "I'm so hungry, I could eat a raccoon!"

"A raccoon," Jamila's mother, Abila said, smiling. "I think the saying is, 'I'm so hungry I could eat a horse.' "

"I know," Cheyenne retorted, "but I couldn't eat a horse! And maybe I could eat a raccoon – it's smaller, you know."

Abila laughed and ushered them through the door into their tidy living room. "Please make yourselves at home while I finish preparing the meal."

Mom and Sage were already sitting on the couch, relaxing while Jamila's dad, Ibrahim, sat nearby, chatting with Mom. He stood and shook Dad's hand as Dad crossed the room, then he nodded to Cheyenne and Skye. "Welcome to our home."

"I'm so glad to be here," Cheyenne said, seating herself politely on the couch beside Mom. She sounded so prim and lady-like that everyone laughed, including Cheyenne. "Well, I am!" she said stoutly, folding her arms in front of her chest, her lower lip sticking out.

"You just love the food," Sage said, betraying her secret.

"So what?" Cheyenne almost shouted. "So do you!"

"So do I," Skye agreed, trying to take her sister's side. "Eating here is like going to a really fancy restaurant."

"Hey!" Mom joked. "What's wrong with my cooking?"

"And mine?" Dad added. "I made the dessert, you know. I took a saskatoon berry pie out of the freezer."

Sage scoffed. "That's one that Kôkom made, not you!"

"Oh well," Dad laughed, turning to Ibrahim. "My mother is a great cook, especially with pies."

"And I brought bannock," Mom added. "What's wrong with my bannock?" She eyed her children sternly, her eyes glittering with laughter.

"Nothing," Skye assured them quickly. "The Hajjars' cooking is just … just—"

"Different," Ibrahim answered for her, smiling her way. "It's kind of exotic, no?"

"Yeah," Sage agreed, "that's it. It's special because we don't get it all the time, like we do Mom and Dad's cooking at home."

"It's novel," Ibrahim chimed in again. He knew all

these important, fancy words since he was a professor at the university, Skye thought.

"Come on," Jamila said, impatiently pulling at Skye's arm. "Come to my bedroom so we can talk in private!" Walking down the hall, the girls entered the room and flopped down on Jamila's neatly made bed. There they stayed, chatting until Jamila's mother called them to the table to eat.

Chapter Eight

Skye didn't have time to think too much about anything until she went to bed. That night, tons of information was dancing in her head. It made sleeping difficult; she just couldn't switch off her mind! Finally, after tossing and turning for what seemed like hours, Skye looked across the room to see the eagle feather shining faintly in the glow of the streetlight streaming through the window. Hopping out of bed, she took the feather off the bulletin board and held it in her hands, carefully caressing it, then rubbing its softness against her cheek.

Her fingers began to tingle with electricity and Skye thought she could hear the sound of a drum beating in the distance. It engulfed her soul, and she closed her eyes, clutching the feather to her chest. Was she going back in time again? Suddenly, the drum became her heartbeat. It beat louder and louder in her chest. She felt the vibrations against her skin, her cheeks, her eyes, and she knew she was living and breathing the sound.

Skye felt her mind begin to whirl. Lights flashed behind her eyelids and she heard the far-off sound of drums growing urgently and more insistently. She twirled faster and faster until everything became one big blur of noise and light. Everything seemed fuzzy and distorted, as once again, Skye slipped back in time.

Skye opened her eyes to find Okômâw hovering nearby, smiling. "I am proud of you, Awâsis," she said, reaching out to touch Skye's cheek. "You are indeed beginning to earn that eagle feather that was gifted to you. You are learning the truth about our people."

"Yes," Skye said quietly. "I wanted to know more."

"That is good, and now you are ready for the next part of your journey."

"Where are we?" Skye asked, looking around. In the distance, she could see a fort made of many tree poles of unpainted wood. The fort's huge wooden gates stood open and a Union Jack flag was flying on a tall pole. Outside the fort, hundreds of her people milled around as if waiting for something. They were standing in groups or sitting quietly on the ground, staring at a big white tent in the distance. The people looked tired, thin and hungry, their tattered clothes hanging on their scrawny bodies, but they were focused on something happening near the fort.

"We are at Fort Carlton," Okômâw replied, keeping a hand on Skye's shoulder. "We are witnessing the signing of Treaty Six, as are all of the people here."

Skye squinted her eyes to see what everyone was looking at. Standing near the white tents was a medicine man. He was praying as the people stood by silently. He smudged with smoke from a small fire and then picked up a pipe and smudged it too. Then he lit it and began praying again. He pointed the pipe slowly up in the air, repeating the process four times, turning and pointing in all four directions.

"What's happening?" Skye asked, struggling to see more clearly.

"It's a pipe ceremony," Okômâw answered, and then Skye recognized it. She had been to pipe ceremonies on her reserve before.

"Our leaders are getting ready to sign Treaty Six," Okômâw added.

Close by, men in black suits and others in uniforms watched too, and Skye knew that they were the Europeans – the Englishmen. They stood near the big white army tent. The medicine man began to sing and pray as the people stood respectfully. Skye scanned the groups closest to the tents. "Those look like the chiefs over there," she told Okômâw. "But they're dressed like the white people – like the army guys," she added, confused.

Okômâw nodded. "The chiefs all received new clothes to wear as part of the treaty signing. That could be because the English wanted to give them a gift; but it could also have been because many of their clothes, made from bison hides, were tattered and worn out."

Skye nodded. That made sense. "Yes, there were no bison around; that's why they signed the Treaty. It was so they could get food, a reserve of land, and education for their families – their children." She studied the serious-looking group of men. "I do like the regalia – the traditional clothes better; they're so bright and colourful. They look worried, Okômâw," Skye added.

"They are worried," Okômâw agreed. "They want to make sure that they make a good deal for their people. It's a big responsibility, especially since there are so many people involved, and the chiefs and English leaders don't speak the same language."

"Ohh..." Skye sighed. "I remember that now. But didn't they have translators to help them?"

"Yes," Okômâw said, "they did. But translators don't always get it right, either. Have you ever read or listened to the wording of Treaty Six?"

"No," Skye replied.

"Well, listen in, Awâsis."

Skye looked up to see an important-looking man unfurl a long piece of paper and begin to read:

"ARTICLES OF A TREATY made and concluded near Carlton on the 23rd day of August and on the 28th day of said month, respectively, and near Fort Pitt on the 9th day of September, in the year of Our Lord one thousand eight hundred and seventy-six, between Her Most Gracious Majesty the Queen of Great Britain and Ireland, by Her Commissioners, the Honourable Alexander Morris, Lieutenant-Governor of the Province of Manitoba and the North-west Territories, and the Honourable James McKay, and the Honourable William Joseph Christie, of the one part, and the Plain and Wood Cree and the other Tribes of Indians, inhabitants of the country within the limits hereinafter defined and described by their Chiefs, chosen and named as hereinafter mentioned, of the other part.

Whereas the Indians inhabiting the said country have, pursuant to an appointment made by the said Commissioners, been convened at meetings at Fort Carlton, Fort Pitt and Battle River, to deliberate upon certain matters of interest to Her Most Gracious Majesty, of the one part, and the said Indians of the other." [1]

---

[1] https://www.aadnc-aandc.gc.ca/eng/1100100028710/1100100028783

"Oh my," Skye breathed, turning to look at Okômâw. "I speak English – or at least I thought I did, until I listened to that. No wonder our people were confused." She frowned in concentration. "I think our people must have signed the Treaty on faith – they trusted that it was a good agreement."

Okômâw nodded. "Yes, I would agree, and it was and is a good agreement. Our chiefs negotiated for a medicine chest to be made available to our people, and also the government was obligated to help our people in hard times – they needed to feed our people if they were hungry. And in return, our people agreed to share the land – to live on reserves of land and, in some cases, to learn how to farm the land."

"So what happened?" Skye asked. "If this was such a great deal, why did our people suffer so much?"

Okômâw sighed. "Because not everyone lived up to the promises that were made."

Skye watched as a long line of chiefs and other important people walked up to sign the document. "But isn't a promise a promise?" she asked, child-like in her anger for her people. "What can we do to help our people?"

Okômâw smiled at her. "That is part of your journey, Awâsis." And she faded away, leaving Skye standing alone at the edge of the ceremony.

Skye awoke with a start, in her bedroom, the

feather resting lightly on her chest. She was angry at what she had witnessed, because she could feel the hopes of all the people. It heated her blood when she thought about how her people had so trustingly signed the treaties, thinking that their lives would improve. But what had happened? she wondered.

It was early morning, and Skye wandered out of her bedroom and into the kitchen in her oversized T-shirt. Dad was sitting at the kitchen table, reading Skye's book. "Good morning, Skye," Dad said. Smiling, he ruffled her already messy hair. "What gets you out of bed so early on a Saturday?"

Skye shrugged, rubbing her cheek against Dad's shoulder. "I couldn't sleep."

"Still having dreams?" Dad sipped his coffee as he searched Skye's face.

She nodded. "Yes, dreams ... or visions," she said, not sure what to call the time-travel experiences she was having with Okômâw. "But they make me ask more questions, you know?"

Dad nodded. "Some dreams do that. They are supposed to make you think and question life."

"So, here's one question," Skye said, pulling a cereal box out of the cupboard and grabbing the milk from the refrigerator. "If signing Treaty Six was so good for our people, what happened?" She dumped cereal into a bowl and added milk.

"Well, mostly, the Indian Act happened," Dad said quietly. He got up and refilled his mug with coffee, stirring in sugar and adding milk. "It's ironic that the signing of Treaty Six and the enactment of the Indian Act happened in the same year – 1876."

"Why?" Skye asked as she shovelled a big spoonful of cereal into her mouth. She was sure hungry after her adventure with Okômâw the night before!

"Well, the Treaty was a contract – a promise to help our people, educate our people and take care of our people if they needed it, to help our people be successful. That's really what the chiefs wanted. They wanted to help their children and grandchildren lead successful lives. The Indian Act took away so many of our rights."

"Really?"

"Yes," Dad continued. "That's why residential schools happened, and the pass system, which forbid our people from leaving their reserves without the permission of the Indian Agent. He was like a guard – a jailer, really. Sometimes our people had nice Indian Agents who helped them, but many times they didn't, and our people felt the brunt – the wrath – of that. The thing is, the Indian Act is still in place today, and it still affects us."

"Hey, you two," Mom said, coming into the kitchen, her voice groggy with sleep. "That conversation is too deep for such a beautiful fall day."

"Yeah," Sage said, traipsing in behind Mom. "Anyway, I need Dad's help today."

"What, Son?" Dad asked, smiling.

"Tryouts for the football team are next week. Will you practise with me? Throw the football wide so I can run to catch it?"

"Sure," Dad agreed. "I'm not very good at it – I never got to play football, but I think I can manage that."

"Yay!" Sage said. "I'm going to make the team and then you can all come and watch me play! And if I do really well, I'll have a really good chance of playing on the junior high school team next year when I'm in Grade 9! I can't wait."

"I wanna come to the games too," Cheyenne said, climbing sleepily onto Dad's lap for a cuddle. "What's for breakfast? I'm hungry."

Suddenly it was a typical Saturday morning, with everyone excited for the day and making plans, calling noisily to one another. Skye sat at the table, the commotion flowing unheeded around her, her mind busily absorbing all of the information Dad had shared with her. She thought about Okômâw too. What had she meant when she said that Skye was earning the eagle feather? Skye knew that in her culture, the eagle feather was presented to people who had done something really important or really special. What had she done?

Nothing, Skye decided, feeling empty inside. She really hadn't done anything, and yet the eagle feather had been gifted to her. Now she felt like she needed to do something to actually earn it.

Chapter Nine

Something grew in Skye over the next few days. She could feel it. It was the need to live up to that eagle feather. But she was only a kid. What could she do?

The question stayed with her for the next few weeks. She thought about it as she sat in school, working on her jellyfish project, doing the computer reading and answering boring questions, and doing more math problems than were required of her.

She thought about it at night, when she sat in her room, reading and studying the books she had borrowed about the history of her people.

Mostly, she thought about it during her sleepless nights, when Okômâw didn't come to her but left her to her own thoughts.

Awaking early the next Sunday morning, Skye got out of bed, dressed and crept into the kitchen. She could tell by the stillness that no one else was up, so she wrote a short note, explaining that she was going for a walk in The Forest. It was there – at the stone – that Skye had received the eagle feather. Maybe returning to that spot would give her some answers.

Propping the note against the coffee machine so her parents would see it first, Skye quietly closed the front door behind herself and escaped into the crisp autumn air.

Fall had come and the leaves on the trees had turned from vibrant green to golden yellow. Many littered the sidewalk where she trod and crunched under her feet, grinding into little bits with her weight. Zipping her jacket against the cool morning air, Skye stepped onto the trail that led to the rubbing stone. A few joggers ran past her, smiling or waving as they went by.

At the stone, Skye stopped, leaning in to run her hands along its smoothed edges. The stone gave her strength. Skye knew, in her culture, stones were very important. Everything had a spirit, including stones.

Circling the rock, she came to the spot where she had fallen asleep that day and the eagle feather had been gifted to her. She waited, expecting that something would happen, but nothing did.

Skye wasn't sure what she was hoping for. An idea, perhaps; a sign; a billboard telling her what she needed to do.

Smiling at her silliness, Skye knew she would not likely get a giant billboard sign saying:

SKYE! THIS IS FOR YOU. HERE IS WHAT YOU MUST DO:

Skye laughed as the image disappeared from her mind and she turned to look toward the river. As she stood taking in the view, she could see people running on the bridge, and kayaks and canoes out on the water. There was something very familiar about this place. Looking around, she chided herself. Of course there was; after all, this was The Forest – her forest.

A sense of déjà vu washed over her as Skye looked across the river to the other side. "Of course!" she cried aloud, clasping her hands together. The first two times she had gone back in time with Okômâw, she had come to this very spot.

She hardly recognized it because the hill wasn't so steep anymore. It had been smoothed out and leveled to make the park. Still, Skye was certain this was the place and it gave her a sense of history; a sense of really belonging. It made everything come alive for her.

After school the next day, Sage found out he made the football team and he was excited beyond belief. He jumped up and down and ran in circles around Skye as they waited for the bus to take them home. "I made it! I made the team!" he yelled as Cheyenne raced up to them. Picking Cheyenne up, he spun her in a wide circle and then plopped her down on the sidewalk.

"More! More!" she begged, lifting her arms to him, but Sage had moved on to Chris, punching him happily on the arm.

"Hey! Cut it out," Chris muttered. "That hurts."

Sage looked upset for a second, then his face cleared as he saw members of the football team wave and point at him on the lawn by the school. "I'll be right back," he said, sprinting toward the other boys.

"You okay?" Jamila asked Chris as he rubbed his arm.

"Yeah," he muttered. "I'm okay."

"Still not happy, though," Skye said, searching Chris' face.

He shrugged his shoulders. "Nah, not really. I'm still not fitting in here. Not like Sage."

"Me either," Skye said. "I still haven't joined any clubs."

The bus pulled up in front of them and the door swung open. "I just wish there was a Powwow Group, you know?" Chris said as he trudged toward the bus. "That's what I really want to do. I just want to dance powwow."

"Yeah, I miss it too," Jamila said, and Cheyenne and Skye agreed.

"Maybe we could just start a group," Cheyenne said brightly over her shoulder as her little legs struggled to mount the bus steps. "I mean, why not?"

"Out of the mouths of babes," Jamila sighed, sliding into the seat beside Skye.

Skye nodded. "It's not as if we haven't tried," she reminded Cheyenne, calling to her across the aisle of the bus. "I tried and Mom tried. What else can we do?"

Cheyenne shrugged her shoulders. "I don't know," she replied, looking Skye square in the eye. "But I know you'll think of something."

Cheyenne's words were like a challenge – a call to action – and they stayed with Skye all evening, swimming inside her brain, interrupting her reading and making her forget what she was saying when she spoke to people.

It wasn't just the words, it was the complete trust and faith Cheyenne had said them with. It was as if she KNEW her big sister could fix this, and that she would.

Cheyenne's unwavering faith scared Skye, but it also ignited a passion in her heart, making her WANT to do something.

"Mom!" Skye called, coming out of her bedroom. "Where are you?"

"Here, in the living room," Mom answered. "I'm watching a movie with Cheyenne." Mom paused the movie as Skye came into the room.

"Do you still have Ms. Ahenakew's cell number? I want to ask her if she knows what happened to all the regalia we had last year."

"Look in my phone," Mom said, handing the cell to Skye. "Just text her and see."

"Thanks." Skye took the phone.

Skye:
> Hi, Ms. Ahenakew, it's Skye Bird. Do you know what happened to all the regalia we had last year?

Rita Ahenakew:
> Hi, Skye! How are you doing? I've been thinking about all of you. I miss our Powwow Group.

Skye:
> Me too. That's why I'm asking about the regalia.

Rita Ahenakew: I have it at my house, in storage. I was waiting to figure out what to do with it. Maybe to find a new Powwow Group. I mean, it belongs to all of us, since we all worked so hard to raise money for it.

Skye: Me, Jamila, Chris and Cheyenne would like ours please.

Rita Ahenakew: Are you starting up a new dance group?

Skye: I'm not sure yet, but I hope so. Also, can you send along the drum Sage used? Thnx.

Rita Ahenakew: Sure, I will make arrangements with your mother next week to deliver it to you.

Skye: Thanks so much!

"Got it solved?" Mom asked as Skye handed back the phone.

"Just for the regalia," Skye said. "Ms. Ahenakew said she would make arrangements with you to get it to us."

"All right, that sounds good," Mom said.

"Yeah," Skye agreed. "I hope it doesn't take too long."

Sage's first big game happened two days later. "You all have to come," Sage announced at breakfast. "It's after school, in the park behind the school."

"We'll be there," Mom laughed.

"Wouldn't miss it for the world," Dad added. "I'll bring chairs and a blanket," he told Mom. "And the pompoms," he teased and Sage punched him on the arm. "All right, all right," he laughed. "I'll leave the pompoms home – this time."

"Daaaad…" Sage wailed. "Cut it out! We don't even own pompoms. And anyway, they're for cheerleaders."

The game was held after school and, judging by the crowd, it looked like most parents had come out to support the junior team. The athletes lined the side of the field, one team on each side. Sage's team wore bright yellow uniforms and the other team wore red and blue uniforms. A whistle blew and members of both teams ran out onto the field and stood in two lines facing each other. Soon they were running all over the field and tackling one another.

"It looks like they just run around for a while and then jump on each other," Cheyenne announced. "It gets kinda boring after a while."

"Don't tell Sage that; he enjoys playing the game."

"Well, he hasn't played yet," Cheyenne observed. "When will he play?"

"I don't know, Apisîs," Mom said. "Soon, I hope."

Many families were crowded up and down the sidelines, sitting on blankets and lawn chairs, and Skye even recognized some of the teachers watching the game as well. She could see Mrs. Miller going from group to group, shaking hands and talking to the parents. She laughed easily and Skye thought it was too bad she didn't smile and laugh more when she saw her at school.

One thing Skye did notice was that Mrs. Miller only walked by her family's blanket quickly, saying hello, but not stopping to chat. Skye wondered if her parents noticed, but she didn't say anything. It felt like a slight or something, or maybe Mrs. Miller was a little shy since she really didn't know the Bird family yet.

Sage didn't play until the very end of the game, and then he was only on for a few minutes. "There he is!" Cheyenne called, jumping up and down. "Go, Sage, go!" Laughing, she clapped her hands and cheered." That's my big brother," she piped up, glancing at the people beside them. "He can sure run fast!"

There were a couple of skirmishes on the field, a few whistles were blown, and then the game was over.

"We won!" Sage yelled, whipping off his helmet as he sprinted toward his family. He slid onto the blanket, piling in between Skye and Cheyenne and rolling around in joy.

The coach blew a long, loud whistle, calling Sage and a few other team members back. "Gotta go!" Sage called, jumping up. "See you soon."

"You didn't get to play much," Cheyenne told him.

Skye could see the hurt in his eyes, but it quickly vanished. "That's just the way it is; I'm the new kid around here and I have to pay my dues, you know."

"What does that mean, 'pay your dues'?" Cheyenne asked, watching as Sage ran back toward his teammates and coach.

"It means he has to wait until the coach thinks he's ready to play," Dad said quietly, and Skye could see that he was unhappy about the situation. "Everyone has to pay their dues at something," he added.

"But that's not right," Skye pointed out, "and it's not fair. Sage isn't the only new kid on that team; and no one should have to pay dues or whatever. Everyone should just get to play, you know?"

"That's the system, My Girl," Dad said, squeezing her shoulder. Skye hated it when Dad talked about the system; it was never fair or equal.

Skye and her family came to three more games and each time was the same; Sage didn't get to play until the very end, and only for a few minutes. Jamila and her parents came to one game and sat with the Bird family. Skye saw Abila put her arm on Mom's and whisper something about equal time on the field for everyone.

Ibrahim was more direct. "I would go talk to the coach if it was me," he said quietly, looking back and forth between Dad and Mom. Dad looked really uncomfortable. "I know it's difficult, believe me," Ibrahim continued. "I – we – our family has seen this kind of thing before. It happened with Marwan, Jamila's brother. It's like nobody really sees it. But actually, they just pretend not to see it so they don't have to deal with it. It's better if you try to handle these things head-on."

Dad nodded, looking at his shoes, and Skye remembered how much Dad hated confrontation. "I'll think about it, Ibrahim," he said quietly, "but I do appreciate your insight, and your friendship," he added, and the men silently clapped one another on the back.

After the third time, Dad went down to have a word with the coach, even though Sage begged him not to. "I'm just going to ask him to give you a little more playing time, Sage," Dad explained. "I mean, you love the game so much and you work so hard at it. It only seems fair."

Dad was down on the sidelines talking to the coach a long time while parents collected their children, gathered up their chairs and blankets and left. He looked good, Skye thought, his long braid hanging neatly over his shoulder, twisting as he turned his head back and forth with the conversation.

"I don't think he's getting very far," Skye commented. She could tell by the hunch of Dad's shoulders that he was frustrated. "What's the big deal, anyway?" she said. "They should just let Sage play," she said as a movement caught the corner of her eye. She looked to see Mrs. Miller hurrying past, head down. Was she avoiding the Bird family?

Mom shrugged, a worried look on her face. "I know they should." Mom's eyes followed Mrs. Miller as she stopped to chat to a group of parents standing nearby and Skye wondered what she was thinking.

"Let's go," Dad called as he came up to them. He quickly gathered up the chairs and headed for the car.

"Well?" Mom asked, her voice unsure.

Dad just shrugged his shoulders, "I talked, but I don't know if the coach really listened." When Cheyenne started to interrupt, Mom just shushed her. "Let's wait for Sage in the car," was all she said. The family trooped quietly out of the park toward their vehicle, each lost in their own thoughts.

It was quiet at home that night and Skye went to bed worrying about all of the unspoken thoughts and words hanging in the air.

On the bus the next morning, Chris and Sage sat behind Skye and Jamila, and Cheyenne sat with Brandi a couple of seats ahead of them. "Nice game," Chris commented, his voice full of sarcasm.

Sage seemed to know exactly what Chris was

getting at. He wasn't pretending anymore. "I can't help it if the coach won't put me on the field."

"Maybe not," Chris said, "but you don't have to be on the team then."

"I like being on the team," Sage retorted, his voice sharp with anger.

"Do you?" Jamila asked softly, turning to look at him. "That coach isn't being fair to you."

"He's not," Skye added pointedly as the school bus pulled up in front of the school.

"But I like being part of the team!" Sage repeated hotly.

"I don't think you're really part of the team." The words jumped out of Skye's mouth before she could stop them.

"Let's face it," Chris said, picking up his school bag and standing in the aisle. "You're just a book-end."

"A bookend?" Sage echoed, confusion written all over his face.

"Yeah, he only plays you at the very end of the game. Did you ever stop to figure out why, Sage?" Chris ground out angrily. "He's using you, that's why. You're a token."

"I am NOT a token!" Sage practically yelled, roughly pushing past Chris and jostling down the aisle and off the bus in a huff.

"He is, you know," Chris muttered, looking at Jamila and Skye. "The coach is just using him."

It made Skye sad to think that, and a little pain erupted in the pit of her stomach. It stayed there all day, festering and swelling every time she thought about Sage.

Chapter Ten

The regalia arrived in long, plastic clothes bags to protect the beautiful tunics and leggings from dust and dirt. "I know you'll take good care of them, Skye," Ms. Ahenakew said as she helped Mom hang the garment bags in the hall closet. "How are you enjoying school?"

Skye shrugged her shoulders. "I miss our old school. I miss you, and I miss all of the things we had there – like our Powwow Group."

"Well, it looks like you're starting up a powwow group at your new school; that's a good sign. You have all of the regalia for now – enough for about twelve kids to wear."

Skye nodded, "Thanks for bringing it over," she said, wondering if the regalia would ever be used again. "How are you liking your new school, Ms. Ahenakew?" she asked, to try to get rid of the sad feeling in the pit of her stomach.

Ms. Ahenakew smiled a tight little smile that

didn't quite reach her eyes. "I'm having trouble adjusting as well," she said. "I know things take time, but I miss our old school too. And I'm only working part-time right now," she added quietly.

"Would you like to stay for coffee?" Mom asked. "I just made fresh bannock."

"Hmm..." Ms. Ahenakew sniffed the air. "I thought I could smell it baking. How can I resist? There's nothing in the world like warm bannock and yours is one of the best I've had!"

It was true. Skye smiled as she watched Ms. Ahenakew follow Mom into the kitchen. Mom's bannock was the best. In the past, she often delivered it to various classes and teachers at the old school.

Skye heard the rattle of coffee mugs and the scrape of chairs, and the anxious tone in Mom's voice as she began to talk about Sage and the football team. "It's not really obvious, except to anyone who might really be paying attention," Mom murmured. "It's one of those things that would be difficult to prove but, as a parent, it eats you up inside."

Everyone was worried about Sage these days and no one seemed to know what to do. Sage just dragged himself around the house like a tired old workhorse, wrapped in a grey cloud of frustration.

That night in bed, sleep eluded Skye, no matter what she did. After tossing and turning for what felt like hours, she finally whispered into the darkness, "What should I do?"

Suddenly the eagle feather seemed to beckon her. Slipping from bed, Skye plucked the feather from the bulletin board, her fingers beginning to tingle with energy. An electrical charge raced up her arms as the tiny hairs stood up on end. Her room began to spin and the faint light from the tiny stars on the ceiling blurred together until Skye felt like she was part of the whirling heavens above. Her feet lifted off the ground and she was spinning through space, the feather still clutched in her fingers as she moved backward through time.

The sound of the drumbeat persisted loudly, reverberating in her ears. Skye could feel its vibration through the soles of her feet. Opening her eyes slowly, she found herself surrounded by many people, and she was confused. They were all wearing modern clothes. They were holding hands and solemnly dancing a round dance, in the middle of a shopping mall. Shocked, Skye took a step back and felt a hand on her shoulder, "It's all right, Awâsis," Okômâw's voice soothed. "You are safe here."

"Where are we?" Skye asked, peering around her.

"I think I recognize this place. I've shopped at this mall."

"Yes, you are familiar with this spot," Okômâw confirmed.

"But what's going on?" Skye asked. She watched as the round dance continued, the people dancing in a large circle as shoppers tried to squeeze around them.

"Perhaps this is one way to make a change," was all Okômâw said, and she held Skye's hand as they stood watching.

Skye wracked her brain, trying to remember what she had seen and heard about this. It finally came to her; this was a public demonstration of a group who wanted to make positive changes. They had found a safe, very open, but profound way to show the world that they were around and that they cared about things. "I understand!" Skye exclaimed, her face beaming with excitement.

Okômâw smiled at her. "But now, what will you do with all of your knowledge?" she asked and disappeared, leaving Skye to puzzle out the answer.

Skye suddenly found herself back in her own room, her body still throbbing from the rhythm of the drum, her mind buzzing with everything that Okômâw had shown and taught her. She knew she would not sleep that night.

Blurry eyed, as the morning sun rose higher in the sky, Skye looked at all of the sheets of paper spread around her room. She had spent the night making lists and making plans.

Things I Need to Help Me Adjust to the New School
- to join a group I like
- a group like Powwow or Culture Club
- to have/make more friends
- to get books for Cheyenne and other little kids in the school library – books about our culture

Things My Friends Need
- the same things as me
- a Powwow Group – Culture Club – drumming group
- to be in the same class, but it's probably a little late to change that now
- to learn about our own culture in class

Ways to Start Making a Change
- start a petition
- how many people would need to sign it? Where do I/we find people? How do I/we explain the issues to them?

- hold a round dance
*Where could we hold a round dance??
**Who would join in the round dance?

Things Needed
- for petition – lots of paper, pens, information about issues and people to help
- round dance – drum and drummer – Would recorded music work?
- people to dance and join in

Skye sighed and looked at her handiwork. Now she just needed to figure out how and when to do something. This was actually a lot harder than it looked! However, she was strong. She would figure out how to do something – and soon. She would start by talking to Jamila.

"Sure, I'll help you!" Jamila agreed, clapping her hands excitedly. "I'm a good organizer, you know."

"I know," Skye agreed with her. "You can keep us organized. You're also a good promoter. You can help me advertise and promote the idea, but only to a few people to start with. We don't want this getting out to the public just yet."

Jamila nodded, "Whatever you say, Boss," she said, making a little salute with her hand touching her forehead. Both girls laughed.

They started with Chris, who was on board right away. "Let's start collecting signatures," he suggested.

"But for what?" Skye asked.

"Well, like you said, what about for getting a powwow dance group going at this school?"

Jamila nodded. "I like the idea. Let's start by talking to all the members of the dance group and see how many signatures we can get. Tonight, let's get together at my house and figure out what the beginning statement will say," she told Skye.

"Statement?" Skye frowned.

"The part that explains why we want people to sign the petition. I don't know exactly, but I do know you need to have that at the beginning of a real petition," Jamila explained.

"Okay," Skye said. "I'm sure my Mom will agree to let me come over for awhile, even if it is a school night."

They met at Jamila's house that night and, between eating squares of aish el-saraya, a sweetened bread pudding that was Jamila's favourite Lebanese dessert, they concentrated on the correct wording for their petition.

"I love that dessert," Skye said, licking the sweetness from her fingers.

"Me too," Jamila said. "My imeh knows it's my favourite," Jamila said, slipping into Arabic for the word 'Mom'. "Sometimes we have it with lots of cream, in a dish, and sometimes it's plain, like tonight. Either way, it's wonderful!"

Skye heartily agreed. "Maybe we could learn how to make this sometime. What do you think?"

Jamila smiled happily. "I'll ask my imeh. I'm sure she'll say yes!

"But let's get to work for now; there's lots to be done."

The girls passed words and phrases back and forth for a long time, trying to come up with the right words. "We don't want to sound snotty," Jamila said.

"No, we don't," Skye agreed, wrinkling her forehead in concentration and crossing out a sentence on her page. "And we don't want to sound like whiny little kids."

"Nope," Jamila agreed. "Read me what we've written so far."

"Okay." Skye picked up the paper and read:

"We, the undersigned, would like to start a Pow-wow Dance Group and/or a Culture Club at our school. If you would be interested in supporting us with this request, please add your name below."

"Do you think we should explain why?" Jamila asked.

"You mean, like saying that we had a group before at our other school?" Skye frowned. "No, I don't think so because it might make new people feel like they can't join since they didn't participate last year."

Jamila nodded, "Yes, you're right."

"Do you think we should include when we'd like to run it – like a day or time – like after school?" Skye wondered, studying the paper.

"Hmmm," Jamila thought. "No, I think that's too much information. We can decide all of that later, once we get approval for our group."

"Hmm…" Skye said, "something is missing, though." Both girls thought for a few minutes, rubbing their foreheads and staring at the paper until their eyes were red and sore.

"I know!" Skye suddenly exclaimed. "I think we should add something like … blah-blah … start a Powwow Group at our school to learn the cultural dances of our Indigenous people and to have fun… What do you think?"

Jamila furled her brow in concentration. "Read the whole thing again, please."

And Skye read, "We, the undersigned, would like to start a Powwow Dance Group and/or a Culture Club at our school, to learn the cultural dances and customs of our Indigenous people, and to have fun! If you would be interested in supporting us with this request, please add your name below."

"I like it!" Jamila cried. "It's perfect!"

They carefully typed the words onto a Word document in the computer, added many lines on the paper for people to fill in their names, and then printed the page many times. Jamila carefully saved the document on the desktop, "in case we need more copies," she said. They watched as the printer spit out the pages.

"I'll take some," Skye said, separating the pages.

"And I'll take some too. We can give some to Chris," Jamila added, "and let's see what happens!"

"How many signatures do you think we'll get?" Skye asked.

"I don't know," Jamila said, "but I'll bet it's lots!"

Jamila was wrong; the girls didn't get as many signatures as they had hoped. Skye cornered several kids in her class, but only four kids signed it. Three were from her school last year – Raven Poorman, Justin Greyeyes, and Tyrell LaVallee – and one was a new kid who said it sounded like a fun thing to do. Jack had signed as well and tried to persuade other kids to sign too, but they wouldn't.

"I should start a petition about wearing hats in school," Tyrell muttered as he scrawled his name on the line.

"Why don't you?" Skye asked.

He looked at her coolly. "I'll wait and see how well you get on with your petition first," he smirked.

"Not that I don't wish you well; I just don't think you'll get very far with it."

"But it's a petition," Skye protested, stacking the pages together and hugging them to her chest. "Don't you have to listen to a petition?"

Tyrell laughed. "What do you think this is, a democracy? I don't think school works that way – at least not this one." Jamming his hat on his head, he strode from the room and out into the hallway.

Chapter Eleven

"Dad, what does 'democracy' mean," Skye asked that night as they were cleaning away the dishes after supper.

Dad raised his eyebrows. "Are you studying forms of government at school?"

"No, it's just a word Tyrell used today and I'm not sure I get what he meant."

"Well, a democracy means the people have the power to make laws or change laws. Canada is a democracy, so when we vote, the votes are counted and the winning political party is the one that has the most votes. That party forms the government and they get the power. They have the right to make decisions.

"That's a simplified version of the word," he concluded.

Skye nodded, "So, with a petition..."

"In that case, you have to get a certain number of signatures before the government will look at an issue."

"Can the government ignore a petition?" Skye wanted to know.

Dad laughed. "It may want to, but if people have gone to the trouble to sign a petition, then it's in the best interest of the government to work with the people to listen to their concerns and make some changes."

"Thanks, Dad," Skye said.

"Thinking of starting a petition?" Dad joked and Skye smiled but remained silent, biting her lip. She didn't know why she didn't want to tell her parents but, for some reason, she needed to keep this a secret, for now.

Skye decided to try to get Miranda on board, even though they hadn't really spoken to one another since the big school move. She waited for Miranda one day after school, watching until her other friends had disappeared down the hallway, calling and laughing to one another.

"Hey, Miranda," Skye greeted, coming up beside her. "Can I get you to sign this petition?"

"What's it for?" Miranda asked, looking some-what interested. "Knowing you, it's probably something to do with our lost culture," she said, her voice snotty.

Skye almost backed down, lowering the page to her side, then she thought of the eagle feather hanging on her bulletin board in her bedroom. "Yeah, so what if it is?" she retorted, trying not to sound angry or defensive. "It's about starting a Pow-wow Dance Group here at this school."

"You can count me out," Miranda said, turning her back on Skye and beginning to edge down the hallway. "There's no way I'm going to dance pow-wow here at this school."

"But I thought you loved it, Miranda," Skye continued. "You sure looked as if you did, and you were so good at it!"

"Well, thanks," Miranda backed down a bit, "but I'm still not signing it. My new friends wouldn't be my friends anymore if I did. They'd think I was weird or something."

Skye just shook her head. "Then they're really not very good friends to you, are they, Miranda?" She watched silently as Miranda whirled around and marched away without saying anything.

Jamila had a few signatures, as did Chris, but it sure didn't add up to much. "Maybe I can get Sage to sign," Skye mushed, studying the list.

Chris shook his head. "I already tried. He almost laughed in my face and told me to just figure out how to fit in at this school."

Skye nodded, her lips pursed together in a straight line. "That sounds exactly like something

Sage would say. He's like a broken record when he talks to me these days, and it's always the same message: Just try to fit in - fit in - fit in," she said, in a singsong voice and sounding exactly like a stuck record.

Everyone laughed and Chris punched her lightly on the arm, "Aren't you the clever one?" he smiled.

"Now what?" Jamila asked.

"I think we should talk to Mrs. Miller. I mean, we have about thirty signatures on the sheet, and that's a lot," Skye said, but her heart pounded loudly in her chest at the mere thought of having to face their principal.

"You're right!" Jamila exclaimed, "I mean, thirty seems like tons to me. I'm sure she'll listen to us."

"Good luck," Chris called, not feeling quite so confident.

"You make the appointment, Jamila," Skye begged. "Since that first day, I'm a little afraid of her."

"Okay," Jamila agreed. She walked up to the assistant's desk and asked to make an appointment, while Skye stood near the door to the library, watching from across the wide lobby.

"Well?" Skye asked when Jamila came bouncing back across the area.

"Our appointment is tomorrow at recess." The bell rang, loud and piercing in Skye's ear, and she winced. "Oh, we've got to go. Let's make some plans on the bus tonight about what to say tomorrow."

"Okay," Skye agreed, and her heart lifted. Mrs.

Miller would have to listen, now that they had so many signatures on the page.

At recess the next morning, Skye met Jamila outside her classroom, her heart pounding loudly in her chest. The pages of the petition were neatly tucked inside a large envelope, along with the notes the girls had made. Skye reached into the envelope with shaking fingers and pulled out the two smaller pages of notes. "Here, let's go over our ideas as we walk," she said. Scanning her notes, Skye added, "You're going to talk first and butter her up a bit, then introduce our idea."

"Yes," Jamila said. "I will say what I practised with you yesterday — how important the groups are to everyone, how much fun they were, and how much we learned about everyone's culture."

"Good," Skye said. "Then I talk about how each club met once a week — Powwow met more often when there was a big powwow or performance coming up — and I'll mention how the Culture Club created the Friendship Night too."

Jamila clapped her hands in excitement as they neared the principal's office. "We've worked so hard on this! It has to work!"

"I hope so," Skye wished fervently, wiping her sweaty fingers on her jeans as Jamila knocked on Mrs. Miller's office door. "I really, really hope so."

Thirty minutes later – long after the recess bell had rung, calling the students back inside – Jamila and Skye emerged from Mrs. Miller's office. Tears pooled in Jamila's eyes. "How could she turn our idea down?" she wondered, her mind shocked and in disbelief.

"I don't know," Skye said, squeezing Jamila's hands tightly. "She didn't even look at the petition to see who'd signed it. It was like she didn't even care."

"I know," Jamila sighed. "I don't feel like she listened to us at all."

"So we failed," Skye mumbled sadly. "I can't believe it. I was so sure it would work."

The girls walked hand-in-hand, slowly down the deserted hallway, pausing near Jamila's classroom door. "Here, you take the signatures," she thrust the envelope into Skye's hands. "I don't want to think about it anymore; it hurts too much."

"Yeah," Skye agreed as she reluctantly took the envelope out of Jamila's outstretched hands. She didn't want it either. They hugged, long and hard, trying to make one another feel better. "At least we tried, Jammi," Skye said, using Jamila's nickname. "Let's remember that." Then more words popped out of Skye's mouth. "That was Plan A," she said, surprising even herself. Where were these words coming from?

"But what's Plan B?" Jamila wanted to know.

"I haven't figured out Plan B ... yet," Skye admitted, but she squared her shoulders and stood up straighter, thinking about the last time she had seen Okômâw. What would Okômâw do in this situation, she wondered. But actually, it didn't really matter what Plan B was, as long as she didn't give up. That was one of the messages Okômâw was trying to share with her.

A little bud of hope and something stronger – something like determination – fluttered to life in the pit of Skye's stomach. "I'll figure out something," she promised, "and soon!"

Jamila nodded and wiped her eyes. "I know you will!"

"Okay," she added, turning reluctantly away. "See you after school."

Skye nodded. "Okay. Bye." She turned away and entered her own classroom door.

Quietly closing the classroom door behind her, Skye walked to her desk, stuffing the envelope inside. Her heart was heavy, but she felt a lightness at the same time – a kind of power; a sort of strength coming from the core of her being. What was it?

Skye wondered, sitting still in her desk and letting that feeling of strength wash over her. It felt good. "You're finding answers, Awâsis," a voice whispered in her ear. "You're growing strong. You are becoming a warrior for our people." Skye smiled. It was

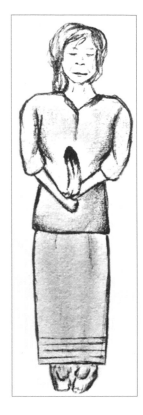

Okômâw's voice, telling Skye she was proud of her, and Skye's heart filled with happiness.

It was announced the next day that parent-student-teacher interviews were going to be held early that year. "It's called 'The Getting to Know You Evening'," Mrs. Bone explained. "This way, teachers, parents, and students can get to know one another. The date for this is two weeks from today, and your parents need to call for a time to see me. Please advise them to phone the school to do so soon. As well, our school superintendent, Mr. Bill Carpenter, will be on hand that evening. He wants to see how we are all doing, so we must make sure to put on our best faces. We want everyone to know how happy we are at our school. Also, I am handing out one of these sheets to each of you to take home." She chose two helpers to hand out the sheets.

When the buff-coloured sheet fell onto Skye's desk, she picked it up and studied it. That name –

Mr. Carpenter – sounded familiar. Skye let that thought slip away as excitement built inside her. This event – The Getting to Know You Evening – was perfect! Skye felt Plan B beginning to fall nicely into place.

Now she just had to convince others of her plan.

Chapter Twelve

Skye called a secret meeting of a few people over the lunch hour the next day. Even though it was cooling off, they met outside, under the big spruce tree on the edge of the playground. That way, they wouldn't be overheard by anyone. She had spread the news through word of mouth and by text, and now Tyrell, Justin, Cheyenne, Brandi, Raven, Chris, and Jamila sat in a circle under the tree.

"So, are you all in?" Skye asked, looking pointedly around the circle at each person.

"I am," Jamila said, "that's for sure. Wow! What a great idea!"

"Me too," Chris agreed, and the others joined in.

"This will be fun!" Brandi clapped her hands in delight, happy to be included.

"I know," Cheyenne agreed.

"We could get into big trouble for this," Tyrell solemnly reminded them.

"But why?" Cheyenne asked. "That doesn't make

sense. I mean, we're only having a dance – a welcome dance."

"Well," Raven said, tousling Cheyenne's black, shiny hair. "Everyone might not see it that way."

"So," Skye continued, "we only have a few days to get this organized. Talk quietly to other people..."

"Like the moccasin telegraph," Justin pointed out and they all laughed.

"Yeah – just like that," Skye said. "If you have something to wear – you know – regalia – that's great. If not, that's okay too. We all know you don't need regalia to be part of this dance."

"I can look at home," Raven said. "I may have something that would fit Brandi."

"Oh, goodie!" Brandi clapped her hands again. "This is going to be so fun!"

The school bell rang in the distance, startling the group. "Remember," Skye added, "this is a secret." She put her fingers to her lips. "No telling anyone." They all raced toward the school, hurrying so they wouldn't be late.

"Wait up," Sage called. Skye and Chris slowed down. "Where were you?" he asked Chris. "I was looking for you."

Chris was silent for a moment and Skye said, "We had a secret meeting. We're planning a dance."

"Dance?" Sage said, his eyes narrowing.

"Yeah," Chris asserted, "and we could use a drummer. Are you interested?"

Sage walked along quietly, thinking, his hands

tucked in the pockets of his jeans. "I'll let you know," was all he said as they got to the door and stepped inside.

As Skye wondered who she could ask to join them, Jack popped up right beside her, almost as if she had dreamed him up. "Hey," she said, smiling, reducing her speed in the hallway so that he would slow down too. "I wanted to ask you something."

Quickly, Skye filled Jack in about the big plan. "So we're looking for people to join us," she finished, hopefully.

"Allies," Jack said, smiling. "You're looking for allies ... and you can count me in. I'll talk to a few of my friends, and my little sisters as well."

"Thanks," Skye smiled. "You're a nice kid."

Jack bowed to the waist, flourishing his arm in the air. "At your service, Madame."

"Class, to your seats now," Mrs. Bone called out and Skye giggled as she slipped into her seat. Looking at the whiteboard, she could see that they were about to start their inquiry presentations and she was third on the list. She smiled, realizing that she wasn't as nervous and scared as she had been that first day of school. She was making a few friends in class now, including Jack, and it felt good. It would be easy to talk about jellyfish, even if they weren't her passion. After all, she had learned some things about jellyfish that she wanted to share with the whole class.

The other person she approached about Plan B was Miranda, and she only did so because she noticed that Miranda was spending a lot of time alone lately at recesses and over the lunch hours. "Hey, Miranda," she said later that afternoon, coming up to stand beside Miranda's desk as everyone scurried about, tidying up the classroom and getting ready to go home for the day.

"What's up?" Miranda quipped, a small smile on her lips.

"I just wanted to tell you about an event we're having," Skye said, then telling Miranda all about the dance they wanted to hold.

Miranda hesitated and looked around the classroom at the girls who used to be her friends. They ignored her as they laughed and joked with one another and made plans to meet after school that day. "You were right," Miranda sighed. "They really aren't my friends. They started making fun of me..." She squared her shoulders and looked Skye in the eye. "Thanks for asking me; I'd love to be part of it."

"Yay!" Skye called, giving Miranda a quick hug. "I'm glad. We used to be friends too, remember?"

"Yeah," Miranda grinned. "How could I forget?"

Later that night, after supper, Sage wandered into Skye's room. "So, I've been thinking about the dance," he began.

"And?" Skye encouraged, "What do you think?"

"I think we do need to take a stand; we do need to make things happen at that school and I'm ready to join you. I'll be the drummer."

"What about football?" she asked.

Sage smiled, "I didn't say I was giving up football! I can do both, you know. And maybe I can figure out a way to get Coach to let me play more, you know."

Skye bounced on her bed, mischief gleaming in her eyes. Grabbing a pillow, she bonked Sage on the head with it. "It's about time you came to your senses!" she called as Sage playfully grabbed the other pillow and hit her back. They rolled onto the bed together, laughing.

"Can I play too?" Cheyenne called from the doorway, an eager smile on her lips.

Two pillows sailed across the room and smacked her, almost knocking her off her feet.

"You're it!" Sage and Skye called out together.

Chapter Thirteen

It was the evening of the Getting To Know You event. It had been difficult getting their parents to leave ahead of them, but Sage convinced them that the parents needed to be at the school first. "We're doing something special," Sage told them, "and anyway, Jamila's parents will pick us up."

Their parents left and Skye pulled open the closet door. "Help me get Cheyenne dressed," Skye called as the doorbell rang. Chris, Miranda and Jamila burst in through the door, with Jamila's parents following closely behind.

"We thought you could use some help getting dressed," Jamila's mother said. Skye smiled gratefully.

"We'd love your help," she told them.

Twenty minutes later, the small group of people stood in the shadows outside the school's front entrance. Sage held his drum. It was circular, about 36 centimetres in diameter, and covered in animal hide. The light-coloured leather was pulled tightly over the shell of the drum and tied behind with pieces of rawhide. On the front side of the leather, an eagle was painted. Sage wore a navy, cotton button shirt with white fringes hanging from the sleeves. They swayed about as he moved. Hanging around his neck was a medallion of an eagle that Dad had given him.

Chris stood next to Sage in his bright blue shirt with tassels hanging from the sleeves and hem. Skye liked how the white tassels looked like little white wisps of cloud against the blue material.

Skye stood, impatiently waiting to enter the large lobby of the school, her heart singing. She loved to dance powwow, and it had been a long time since she had danced.

She loved the sound of the drums beating in her ears. She loved the feel of her feet as she skipped and hopped around the circle. She loved the flash and blur of bright colours as the other members of her dance troupe dipped and whirled around her. Most of all, she loved the feel of her dress swaying as her body moved in time to the music. It was the softest and most beautiful dress she had ever worn, and Skye loved it.

Skye was a jingle dancer. Her dress was made of Skye's favourite colours – soft rose and powder blue, almost the colour of the morning sky. Skye felt like she danced among the stars when she danced in it. In addition, several rows of small pieces of rolled tin encircled the front and back of the dress.

They jiggled and clinked together whenever Skye moved, making a cacophony of sounds that could only be classed as noise – a beautiful noise. On her head, Skye wore a matching beaded headband, with a white feather stuck in the back.

Cheyenne stood timidly beside Skye in a similar dress, only hers was bright yellow, and Cheyenne adored it. Jamila was a fancy dancer and her regalia was the brightest yet. It was a vivid purple colour with several rows of white and blue fringes which hung from the shoulders and waist and swayed whenever she moved. Right now, as she spread her arms wide and twirled, the material fluttered and flapped around her in a cascade of colour.

Miranda stood quietly by, dressed in her traditional regalia, holding a fan. "You look beautiful," Skye told her.

"Thanks," Miranda murmured. "I'm really nervous. Should we be doing this?" she asked, looking as if she was ready to flee into the night.

"I'm nervous too," Cheyenne piped up, wiping her sweaty hands together. "What if we get into big trouble?"

"We all know the risk," Chris replied, his voice strong. "How else do we make change?"

"I don't care about getting into trouble," Jamila retorted. "We aren't doing anything wrong, really." But her voice was hesitant. "I mean ... if my parents thought it was really bad, they wouldn't let me do it, would they?"

"I'm still scared," Miranda said.

"I'm scared too," Skye admitted, feeling her blood pounding throughout her body. "I just know this is something we – I – have to do. So, are you with me or not?"

The silence stretched into the shadows as Skye waited, holding her breath. She wouldn't blame her friends if they walked away. After all, she was asking a lot of them.

Slowly, the small group gathered closely around Skye. "We're all in this together," Sage said stoutly.

"Yeah," Chris agreed. "Let's go do this!"

They all looked wonderful, and strong – in spite of the nervousness that Skye still saw in their faces. They were doing this not only for her, but for everyone. She clasped her hands together in happiness, blinking back tears. "It's time!" she called, blood pounding through her limbs. "Let's go."

The small group walked as quickly and quietly as possible – from the evening air into the brightly lit, empty lobby at the front of the school.

Jamila's parents went to join the other parents in the gym, but not before giving them all a quick hug. Skye could see some of her classmates in the gym as well, and a couple of them started walking toward her, curious about what she was wearing.

The small group of six dancers, dressed in their regalia, made a circle ... but even before Sage could begin to beat the drum, several other people – including Tyrell, Justin, Raven, and Skye's new friend Jack – joined the circle. Now the group contained about fifteen people and Skye felt braver seeing Jack smiling widely across the circle from her, holding the hands of his two little sisters. The rest of Skye's little group saw their supporters and grew in confidence too, squaring their shoulders, proud of themselves.

Turning her head, Skye nodded at Sage to begin. Holding the drum up, Sage tested it a few times with soft little taps, then began to beat out a loud and steady rhythm. The group stood still, catching the beat. Everyone bobbed to the drumbeat, waiting until Skye took the first step. Suddenly, they all grabbed hands and began to move – sidestepping and bobbing in a small circle in the centre of the school lobby, in time to the beat of the drum.

The drum rang out, its heavy sound filling her soul, and Skye let herself get lost in the music. It helped her forget her troubles for awhile. When the music pounded inside her, joy bubbled up and ran out of her like a waterfall. The music always made her heart glad.

Sometimes the drumbeat seemed to carry her away to faraway places. Then her feet became so light that she felt like her toes didn't even touch the floor. When that happened, Skye felt as free as a bird, and she imagined herself soaring high above the clouds, leaving the world behind. This is what it felt like whenever Skye danced powwow, but this round dance was different. It wasn't joy Skye felt so much, but a fierce determination to make a change for herself and her friends – for all the kids at this school.

Parents, teachers, and more kids began to gather around, watching as the circle of dancers moved in time to Sage's drum. They thought it was a performance and they stood by, just watching. What should she do? Skye wondered. But Chris and Jamila figured it out. They started smiling and reaching out, beckoning to people to join the circle and dance.

Slowly but steadily, the small group of dancers grew ... and grew. More and more people followed the sound of the drum and joined the round dance, and Skye's heart soared with happiness. This was exactly what she wanted to happen.

She saw her parents come into view, their faces wide with surprise. They too soon joined the circle, making sure to get right between Skye and Cheyenne. Dad gave Skye a quick little one-armed hug and winked at her. "I should have figured you'd be up to something," was all he said.

"Did the principal know about this?" Mom demanded, her eyes filled with concern, but nothing was bothering Skye now. She just shook her head. "What are you doing?" Mom cried, and Skye knew she was worried about the consequences later.

Skye just smiled. She had not a care in the world. "Dancing," was all she said. "I'm dancing."

Mom blinked back tears and squeezed her hand so tightly that Skye thought it might fall off. "Way to go, My Girl," Mom whispered. "I'm so proud of you!"

Then Skye saw Mrs. Bone tentatively join the group, grasping Justin's hand on one side, and

Raven's on the other. "Wow," Skye said, tears suddenly gathering in her eyes. She got Jamila's attention, "Look who just joined the dance."

"That's nice," Jamila commented. "My teacher's dancing too," she said, nodding in that direction. "And so is the librarian, Mrs. Greenwood."

"I never even knew her name," Skye said. "I'm glad she's dancing."

"Yes," Mom added. "As far as I can tell, it looks like almost all the staff have joined in the round dance." Even Sage's coach, who had been leaning against the gym door, watching, finally broke into the circle and danced.

From the far corner of the room, Skye saw Mrs. Miller come out of the gym, a horrified and angry look on her face. Then Skye saw Mr. Carpenter

behind Mrs. Miller. Skye recognized him as the man who had once been her principal and she almost jumped for joy. He was beaming at her – at the whole group.

Walking toward the circle, he reached over, shook Dad's hand and then took Skye's sweating fingers in his. "I remember you," he said, smiling at her. "I remember that you always loved to dance powwow. You know what? I love to dance too!"

Skye's happiness overflowed and she felt her heart soar above the crowded school. There were still people pressed into the back corners, watching, and Skye was sure she saw Okômâw grinning at her from the far reaches of the room. Could it be? she wondered. She squinted her eyes, peering to see, but Okômâw was gone.

By the time Sage brought the dance to an end, with the double loud beat of the drum, the circle was so large it was touching the walls of the lobby. Whenever Skye went past the library door, her sleeves rubbed against it, and people couldn't get out of the gym unless they broke into the middle of the circle, which no one did.

Clapping and cheering erupted and then Mr. Carpenter called for quiet. "What a great way to end this evening!" he called out so that everyone could hear. "And you have such a fine-looking Powwow Group." He looked down at Skye, Jamila, Cheyenne, Chris, and Miranda – all dressed in regalia, their cheeks and foreheads shiny with perspiration.

"I was going to make a little speech tonight, to welcome everyone to this new schooling situation, but it looks like this fine dance group has done it for us and now I don't need to." Several parents chuckled and looked relieved that they wouldn't have to stay too much longer and listen to speeches. "I encourage more of you students to join the Powwow Dance Group and the Drumming Club," he said, looking over and nodding at Sage. "At my former school, many students, no matter what their heritage, belonged to the Drumming Club and the Powwow Group as well. It's a wonderful way to get to know a different culture – in this case, our Cree culture. For we all know this school stands on Treaty Six Territory, and the homeland of the Métis.

"I want to thank everyone for coming tonight. I don't know if Mrs. Miller has anything to add..." he looked over at her, as did almost everyone, but she merely shook her head, her lips tightly pursed together. "Well, then ... good night!"

A few people clapped, then parents began rounding up children and heading out into the evening air.

"Well done!" Mr. Carpenter congratulated the small Powwow Group. "How is the club going?" he asked.

Skye shrugged her shoulders as Mrs. Miller squeezed in beside her. "Actually, we don't have a Powwow Group at this school—" she began. Then she saw the look on Mr. Carpenter's face. "I ... uhh ... I mean, we are having trouble finding someone who could lead such a group..." Her voice trailed away.

"Ms. Ahenakew was our powwow instructor last year," Sage broke in, still holding his drum.

"I heard that she isn't working full-time this year," Mom added hopefully.

"Well then," Mr. Carpenter smiled, rubbing his hands together. "I will speak to her first thing in the morning. I'm sure she'll be happy to fill in the rest of her teaching contract at this fine school."

"It's all settled then," Mrs. Miller said lamely. Then Mr. Carpenter said to Mrs. Miller, "Let's go into your office and talk about other ways to welcome the new students."

After they left, the little dance group cheered and jumped up and down. "Yay!" Cheyenne and Skye said, their jingles clattering and dancing in delight.

"But Skye should get credit for doing all of this," Jamila said, looking sadly at Skye.

"Yeah," Chris added. "From where I stand, it looks like Ol' Miller is gonna get all the credit for starting something that wasn't even her idea!"

Dad shrugged his shoulders. "Does it really matter who gets credit? Isn't it more about actually getting a Powwow and Drumming Group going here at this school?"

"Yeppers," Cheyenne said, a big yawn escaping from her open mouth. "Now can we go home? I'm exhausted!"

Two Weeks Later

An announcement came over the loudspeaker just before morning recess:

"For all of those students who are interested, Powwow and Drumming Group will start today at noon. Please meet in the library as soon as the bell rings!"

The bell rang immediately after the message and Skye shot up from her seat. Grabbing her lunch bag, she quickly shouldered her way out of the room, Jack following at her heels. "Hey! Wait up!" he called, "I'm coming too." When Skye looked back, she noticed many other students from her class tagging along with Jack. Her heart filled with happiness.

Mrs. Greenwood was in the library, helping Ms. Ahenakew move tables together and make a list of the interested students. She caught Skye's eye across the room and beckoned her over. "You know, Skye, I owe you an apology," she said, her blue eyes very serious. "I thought I was doing the right thing by not having certain books in our library. I thought I was protecting you students by not having you read about certain topics." She cleared her throat. "I am just now beginning to understand why I need to have books on hand – books about our true history, books about residential schools – Ms. Ahenakew is helping me understand." She smiled across the room at her. "I will make sure I have books representing your culture and heritage, and that's a promise ... and if you have any ideas for book titles—"

"Oh, I do!" Skye interrupted. "Thank you, Mrs. Greenwood. That means a lot."

In bed that night, Skye had so much to think about that it was hard to turn off her brain and go to sleep.

Thirty kids had joined the Powwow and Drumming Group! That was a first, and it was wonderful to see. They were already making plans with Ms. Ahenakew about when their first performance would be.

Even Mrs. Bone came to the group's first meeting. Later, she pulled Skye aside. "I understand you dance tap and jazz as well as powwow," she said.

"I do," Skye replied.

"I wondered if you'd be interested in joining the drama club," Mrs. Bone inquired. "We're planning to put on a musical this year and I need dancers."

Skye smiled. "I'd like that," she said, and she meant it.

Skye thought about her busy day, then fell asleep, dreaming about dancing. In her dream, Okômâw appeared, smiling at her – just as she had done at school during the round dance.

In her hand, Okômâw held the eagle feather she had given Skye – only it looked different. It had a long piece of thin leather wrapped around its shaft. Two long tassels hung from it, and Skye knew that they would twirl and spin when the feather moved. The leather piece was sewn with tiny colourful beads and the tassels had puffs of white bird feathers – like pompoms – on the ends. Skye smiled in her sleep. She knew Okômâw was giving her another idea – a way to use that eagle feather. Skye could hardly wait until the next time she danced in her regalia.

Books Mentioned in This Story and Other Books to Look For

1491 – Charles C. Mann
Before Columbus: The Americas of 1491 – Charles C. Mann
Kookum's Red Shoes – Peter Eyvindson
My Name is Not Easy – Debby Dahl Edwardson
Nobody Cries at Bingo – Dawn Dumont
Red Parka Mary – Peter Eyvindson
Road Allowance Kitten – Wilfred Burton
Walk Two Moons -- Sharon Creech
What's the Most Beautful Thing You Know About Horses – Richard van Camp
When We Were Alone – David Alexander Robertson

Acknowledgements

This book would not have been possible without the help of so many people. Thank you to Val Harper, who taught me well, included me in so many ways and introduced me to students and teachers at Mistawasis First Nation. She asked me, many times, to consider writing a book such as this, for all Treaty children.

Many thanks to Amy Basaraba for our many talks and for mentoring me spiritually and in cultural ways. Amy helped me shape this story. Heartfelt gratitude to Lloyd Laliberte for reading the manuscript so thoroughly and helping me with cultural content, advising me about the Cree language and clearing up assumptions. Lloyd made this book that much better. Thanks to Joanna Landry for reading the manuscript through a cultural lens and providing her kind words about the story. Thank you to Debra Heinrichs and Dani Driver for reading the manuscript and offering ideas and suggestions as well as editing. A huge heartfelt thank you to my editor and friend Deana Driver for everything she does to ensure our books are the best! As always, thank you to my wonderful family for their continued love and support.

About the Author

Mary Harelkin Bishop

Mary Harelkin Bishop has been a writer since she was nine years old. She is the author of the best-selling *Tunnels of Moose Jaw Adventures* books, the award-winning *Mistasinîy: Buffalo Rubbing Stone, Seeds of Hope, Gina's Wheels, and Moving Forward: The Journey of Paralympian Colette Bourgonje*. She has also been a teacher, a teacher-librarian, and an educational, instructional consultant with Saskatoon Public Schools, and has spent more than half her career working in core neighbourhood schools. A few years ago, Mary took a leave of absence to study the effects of colonization on Indigenous students in our school systems. Her thesis is entitled: *Soul-to-Soul: Deconstructing Deficit Thinking in the Classroom*. Her newest novels, *Skye Bird and the Eagle Feather* and *Mistasinîy: Buffalo Rubbing Stone*, reflect her learning as she, too, walks with our cousins on the journey toward relationships and reconciliation.

About the Illustrator

Heaven Starr

Heaven Starr is a Dakota Cree woman who lives on Starblanket First Nation in east central Saskatchewan. She started drawing and painting in 2014, in her Grade 10 school year, after learning more about her First Nations background. Her hope is that her artwork will honour her ancestors and bloodlines. She walks, speaks, and prays in life, hoping to make a positive change with whatever she does.